WRONGLAND

Gazmend Kapllani

Translated by Peter Bien

egret fiction | Chapel Hill, North Carolina

Cover and book design by Maxine Mills

Printed in the United States of America

First Edition

PUBLISHER CATALOGING-IN-PUBLICATION DATA

Names: Kaplani, Gkazment, 1967 — author. | Bien, Peter — translator.

Title: Wrongland / Translated by Peter Bien.

Description: Chapel Hill, North Carolina : egret fiction, 2024.

Other titles: Prose works. English.

Identifiers: LCCN 2024931944 | ISBN 9781942281412

Classification: LCC PA5638.21.A65 L3813 2024
DDC ________________

Laertes

www.laertesbooks.org

Grant me the strength to forgive.

Because whoever forgives is the greatest of all.

Because I know I cannot forget.

Meša Selimović, *Death and the Dervish*

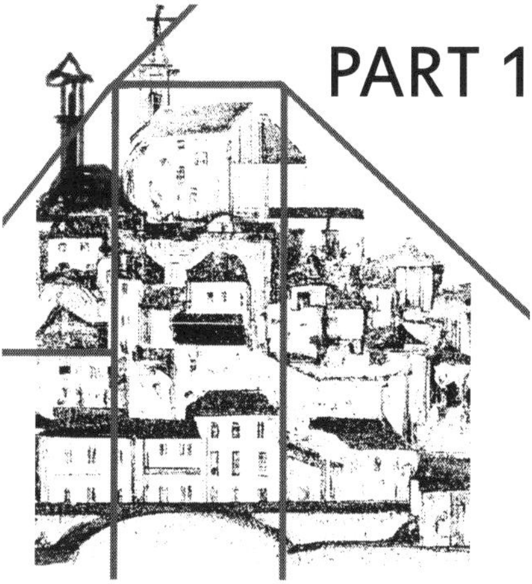

PART 1

1

When he reached the Great Square of Ters,[1] Karl focused on a minaret rising toward heaven on the horizon like a white spacecraft made of concrete. Its construction had begun shortly before he left for Greece. "I'll return in six months," he told his father and brother then. They looked at him as though he were going to the moon, not believing he would return in six months. Nor did he himself believe he would; he said it simply from necessity — and naturally did not keep his promise. His brother Frederik had embraced him with tears in his eyes while his father gazed at him distrustfully, as usual. This time, however, Karl would not meet the distrustful gaze. Twenty-seven years had passed between the day he said he was leaving and his return now to his birthplace, his purpose being to accompany his deceased father to his grave in the city's cemetery, which he had last visited a few days before he crossed the border into Greece. His purpose then was to leave flowers at his mother's tomb and to light a candle there. She had died a year before Karl abandoned the city. The official cause the family gave was a heart attack, but the entire city learned that she had committed suicide, since nothing like that could remain secret in this place where people gossiped even about holes in their neighbors' underwear.

1. In Albanian, "ters" means "jinxed" but also "grumpy," "cranky," "wayward," "gruff." No city with such a name exists in Albania. Ters is the author's mythic invention.

Hearing church bells ringing, Karl looked around as if he had just awakened from a dream. Crossing the Avenue de l'Europe, the city's main street, the first things that impressed him (once again) were the malformed buildings. To the avenue's left and right the ugly apartment blocks constructed during the communist era looked like a beggar's face stung by wasps. Additional floors, added later, rose like repairs on top of old floors, their balconies sticking out like bumps. These recently constructed multistory buildings strove to devour every centimeter of greenery and to stretch out toward the sky like towering stalks of bamboo. Beneath their shadows, the older worn-out blocks of apartments looked like compressed midgets.

Ters, the origin of whose name caused innumerable arguments among local historians, was a peculiar city beginning with the fact that it consisted of two cities in one. The old portion, built of stone totally unchanged throughout the passage of time, stood on top of a rocky hill. The new portion, called the Desert City, stretched out over the flatland below. These two-cities-in-one were separated by a river whose real name was the Skamandros, although the inhabitants nicknamed it La Seine. Ters was a city in which everything — religions, people's names, streets, animals, inanimate objects — existed in double or triple versions.

● ■ ●

Passersby were crossing the Great Square during these early morning hours. Karl did not know anyone who walked in front of him. The younger were probably infants when he departed Ters or, more likely, were not born until after his departure. The older seemed to have the faces of actors in the black-and-white movies he had viewed somewhere, sometime. Seeing these faces of fellow Tersians either fully or half unknown, seeing the malformed buildings and the unchanged Great Square, Karl felt himself dangling in midair, a foreigner in his native city, a native in some foreign city.

Among the Tersians crossing the Great Square, he recognized only Crazy Pandi, who had remained unforgettable in the city's memory after he stood dead drunk one day in the middle of the Great Square, posing as something between a tenor and a wild turkey, to sing L'Internationale, screeching with his entire being, "Arise, comrades of our Ters, let us build walls from Ters to Berlin on and on, walls of hatred and walls of stone." Arrested the same day, he was not seen again in Ters for ten entire years. Yet the verse he sang, that "Debout, les camarades de notre Ters," became a knockout. In cafés the most courageous Tersians sang it sotto voce like conspirators, collapsing from laughter. But the city's police informers, resembling canine fanciers training their bulldogs, sharpened their ears to eavesdrop and, wide awake while the whole city slumbered, expanded their lists of "internal enemies" with new Tersian names.

When Crazy Pandi returned to Ters ten years later, he was prematurely stooped and aged. Not only did he no longer sing, he no longer uttered speech. Not a single letter of the alphabet issued any longer from his mouth. He just set himself up each day like a speechless ruin at the

Slaughterhouse Bossio, next to the city's cemetery, and sold funereal carnations. Some said that he had been tortured with electric shock in dark cells and interrogators' offices. Others went further, spreading word that his tongue had been cut out. In either case, it was clear that stooping Pandi, malformed like the structures of the new city, was able after the fall of communism to extend his sale of carnations to the city's central streets.

• ■ •

Karl was awaited in the family apartment by his father's mortal remains. People were going in and out. The odor of cigarette smoke that issued through the open front door reached the building's entrance three floors below. One of the neighbors recognized him on the stairway and extended his hand: "Mr. Karl, my condolences upon the death of your father. Long life to you, to remember him," he said. Karl took the neighbor's hand in his own hands, as one receives an unexpected gift. He was impressed that the neighbor had addressed him as Mister. "Thank you," he said in a surprised voice. Taking two or three steps, he crossed the threshold carrying his black valise.

His brother Frederik appeared in the corridor. They embraced without sharing a single word. Frederik's eyes were red and swollen from tears and lack of sleep. Karl's eyes were the same, but only from lack of sleep. He had not managed to issue even one teardrop since learning of his father's demise. During this long journey — Boston, Rome, Tirana, Ters — a voice inside him kept persistently whispering, "You should weep;

you have lost your father." The voice complained all the more intensely as the hours passed. It was scandalized when it saw that not only did he fail to weep but that he was absorbed in leafing through various newspapers — The New York Times, The San Francisco Times. He kept reading whatever contained the word "Times." Only when he began to peruse a fashion magazine did his censorious inner voice explode: "How is it possible for me to waste my time with naked female limbs on the day my father died!" One of the women pictured in the magazine resembled his mother. Everyone told him that he looked like his mother, had taken her smile. "How would my life be if I'd been born a woman?" he wondered.

• ■ •

The coffin lay upon a white marble table in the middle of the sitting room, surrounded by multicolored bouquets. Black-dressed women sat in a circle of all-black wooden chairs, holding porcelain coffee cups. They were going to spend the night around the coffin, drink Turkish coffee, read the signs of fate in its dregs, and remain continually awake to guard the corpse from abduction by evil spirits.

Karl's aunt, a woman in good shape despite her 80 years, stood up and hugged him. "May you have his blessing," she said, kissing his cheek. The other women in the circle all rose as a sign of respect. One of them whispered (loud enough for her words to reach Karl's ears), "It's the older son, from America."

Karl turned toward the coffin and, extending his arm, touched it lightly with his fingertips as though wishing to inform it, "I am here."

Afterwards he headed for the adjoining room.

• ■ •

Cigarette smoke spread like a cloud in this room filled with visiting men, somewhat blurring their faces. Karl sat at the room's front in a vacant wooden chair next to his brother, who began to introduce the visitors to him: Jani, the well-known former distributor of lumber; Meti, the premier baker and roaster of at least half the full pans of the city's baklavas each New Year's Day (unemployed now, since no one had any further need of his skills after the fall of the communist regime); Ismael, his father's colleague, a retired former high school mathematics teacher. The remaining visitors in this room belonged to another era called "that time" by everyone: "Fatjon, son of Sheme," said Frederik, indicating with his hand a young man with a skinny face, brown hair, and lively eyes. Karl, shaking hands with the son of Sheme, the city's once well-known lumberman, remembered that Sheme had died when struck by lightning. From that day onward the Tersians considered their two greatest threats and misfortunes to be the evil eye and lightning.

Karl placed his hand over his heart as an indication of gratitude toward the visitors. As he heard the names and saw the faces all around the room, his memory began to open like a drawer filled with old photographs. He thought how well acquainted the people in that room were with the rituals of death. They had attended so many funerals in their lives! Deaths and weddings were the central pillars of social ritual in Ters, as they were everywhere else in the world. Although participation in weddings took place by invitation, in death the home remained open to everyone: rich and poor, influentials and beggars. In this small city where people were born unequal, where they lived unequal and died unequal, death was like a homeland that welcomed all of them with pleasure as equal. Karl remembered an expression of Joseph Roth's when Roth had visited Albania in 1927: "In no other place in the world does death find itself so close to life as it does here."

When I saw Karl I wept . . . tears of lamentation for our father's death . . . emotional tears of a brother seeing the other brother return home after so very long . . . Yet very soon I started to feel puzzled. It happens like this every time, even now when we meet each other so seldom . . . I'm not blind, I see it, feel the invisible wall that rises between Karl and me. That wall has been there for years now. I haven't done anything to build it. If it were up to me, I would now demolish it. Karl was the one who built this wall and Karl is the one who maintains it. The primary material of its construction is Karl's disdain for me. He does not show this openly, of course. Yet I see it in his look, hear it in his silence, comprehend it in his gestures, feel it in the distance he keeps from me . . .

• 2 •

Probably because of an abhorrence that Karl developed during the communist period, rites and rituals did not appeal to him, starting with his own household. His father was one of the few Albanians who had studied as a youth at Moscow's famous Marx-Engels-Lenin Institute. He taught Marxism and Leninism. Karl's name of course honored Karl Marx and his brother's name honored Friedrich Engels.

Everyone in Ters both young and old knew the history of the two brothers' names. Karl, the older one, was born in September 1968, the exact moment when the regime decreed the prohibition of religion and also of all foreign names. That was why the director of the city's Registry of Births and Deaths, Lutfi S., initially refused the name Karl for the newborn infant. "I have orders from the government, comrade Omer," he said over and over again to the father who was frowning from distress, "orders that no imported name be accepted." This question of the name Karl became still more complicated since, in agreement with a circular that had arrived at the Registry just a few weeks before the child's birth, the names of the leaders of Marxism-Leninism were strictly forbidden to be given to common mortals. Lutfi S. zealously explained that this was a wise and precautionary measure whose purpose was to prevent any possible profanation of the sacred names. "You yourself, comrade Omer, know the case of that Lenin from Ters who was arrested two years ago for hostile action against the people's authority," he added with his permanently servile expression. The vexed father replied, "In other words, comrade Lutfi, are you hinting that my son may become an enemy of the Party and the Nation?" Lutfi S., gathering himself together then like a hedgehog being stoned, said, "Alas, comrade Omer, we consider you to be the Party's light in Ters, but that name will cost me my livelihood. Bring me a written document from the government and I'll record the name in a flash."

The "record-the-name/cannot-do-so" controversy between the Registry's director and Karl's father lasted about a year. "Our son is like Odysseus; he is 'Outis' ('No-name') in the Cyclops' cave," said Vali, the baby's mother, her eyes filling with sorrow. Omer M., with unspeakable persistence for a full year, kept sending letters to members of the Politburo in Tirana as well as specifically to Enver H., the Eternal and Unmistakable Leader, begging them to let the name Karl be given to his son — until one day the miracle happened: a personally handwritten epistle signed by Enver H. reached the trembling hands of Omer M. "You, an unbending communist who has distinguished himself in the implacable class struggle and in the imposition of the dictatorship of the proletariat, have every ethical and legal right to give to your beloved son, that future soldier of the Party and the Nation, the name of the great teacher and leader of us all, Karl Marx," wrote Enver H., among other things. In a matter of just a few hours the letter acquired mythical significance in Ters. No other Tersian had ever received a communication written by the personal hand of the dictator. For this reason Lutfi S., as soon as he became informed, did not even wait for Omer M. to appear at the Tersian Registry's door. He himself ran huffing and puffing to the Marxism-Leninism teacher's apartment carrying in his hands the massive Registry book. In this servile fashion he recorded the name Karl and signed for it while incessantly repeating the sentence, "May your Karl live well and achieve great things, comrade Omer." When Karl's brother was born two years later, Lutfi S. offered absolutely no objection. He recorded the name Frederik, drenching the child's father with compliments and genuflections.

Troubles began regarding Karl himself, however, as soon as the naming adventure concluded. Children's arguments in the neighborhood often became an occasion for him to feel his name a curse. To tease him, other children deformed his name from Karl to Kar.[2] Many times during his childhood this perverse play on words made him bite his lips and weep from rage. The abuse grew less with the passage of years, but the moment when Karl truly felt delivered from the weight of his name did not come until he had crossed the Greek frontier.

• ■ •

Family members' birthdays were not the only ones celebrated with ritualistic respect in their home; Marx's birthday was celebrated as well (Engels's was not considered so important). On Marx's, Karl and Frederik read excerpts from the *Communist Manifesto*. Karl still remembered the first paragraph

2. "Penis" in Albanian.

by heart: "A specter is haunting Europe — the specter of communism. All the powers of old Europe have entered into a holy alliance to exorcise this specter: Pope and Tsar, Metternich and Guizot, French Radicals and German police-spies." The two small brothers recited without understanding the meaning. They did so nevertheless with great appetite because the reading of the *Communist Manifesto* brought as reward the applause of their parents and, best of all, sweets.

After Karl and Frederik finished the recitation, their mother, a geography teacher, showed them, on an old multicolored European map, Marx's and Engels's wanderings over the continent — Berlin, Manchester, Paris, Brussels, London.

"Why don't we take the same journey as Uncle Marx?" Karl once asked his parents. His mother smiled with embarrassment and did not answer. His father then intervened to explain that Karl Marx would never have moved from his birthplace if the bloodthirsty bourgeois and corrupt clergy had not persecuted him and forced him to become a refugee without a homeland. "But we in our socialistic homeland lack nothing; we are not persecuted by anybody; we have no need to go anywhere." He always concluded this sermon of his in the same serious Sunday School style, without the slightest trace of irony, stressing the words "nothing," "anybody," and "anywhere" in particular. Each time the episode entered Karl's mind he felt something between hilarity and scorn. He had not managed to understand whether his father was consciously fibbing or actually believed this drivel.

• ■ •

Karl resented his reading from the *Communist Manifesto* more and more as he grew older until one day he revolted against the ritual and declared, "I do not want to read!" His father looked at him with surprise at first. His mother and his brother Frederik looked at him with terror. Father then asked him in a harsh voice to change his mind, then ordered him to read, this time in a voice that, despite its effort to sound commanding, betrayed confusion, an imperceptible quiver that only Karl was in a position to register. This quiver in Father's voice gave Karl an inexplicable, almost savage pleasure, making him still more obstinate. "Why don't you want to read?" Father then asked him, showing himself resigned. "I don't want to!" answered Karl, curtly. At the end, Frederik recited alone. Unlike Karl, he never opposed his father's will, never called into question any paternal exhortation, wish, or command.

That was the last time they celebrated Marx's birthday in their home. Karl was 13 years old. His refusal to read was his first rebellion against an established ritual. At the same time there was also an unconscious declaration of war against paternal power. That day something in the father-son relationship broke. With the passage of time, this break would become an abysmal chasm.

An absurd fear often invades my mind: that Karl may someday commit suicide . . . a fear that has been secretly eating away at me for many years after the day when our mother did commit suicide . . . No matter how infrequently I see Karl — more and more infrequently — that fear follows close behind me. . . . Especially when I find myself down there in the morgue, my thoughts go unintentionally to our mother and to Karl . . . to both together, simultaneously . . . and then the fear leaps up from the darkness like a ghost and comes to sit cross-legged in my brain . . .

•3•

At 2 a.m., when visitors stopped coming, Karl and Frederik went to the kitchen to eat cheese pies and spinach pies cooked by their neighbors in the apartment house.

Frederik then began to explain to Karl the next day's funeral arrangements.

"I've spoken to the hodja. He'll be there at ten o'clock in the morning.

"To the hodja?" Karl repeated, to be certain he had understood correctly.

His brother shook his head in a manner indicating that Karl, having been away for such a long time, had not become aware of important changes in their father's life. Frederik told him immediately that their father had devoted himself to religion during the last few years and had become an observant Muslim. Before his illness he was even thinking of performing the hadj to Mecca.

Father at one time had been an inexorable atheist, serving then as chief of a journey to delirium by a multitude of young men and women brandishing pickaxes and sledgehammers in the air like ecclesiastical icons in ceremonies of exorcism. Shrieking the slogan "Religion is the opium of the masses," they had climbed the hill of Ters's old city and had demolished the Islamic mosque and monastery, the Orthodox and Catholic churches, and the Sephardic synagogue. Now, as was obvious, Father had crossed to the opposite side, had defected to the believers. He always needed to believe in something absolute, Karl thought. Or was his turn toward God perhaps a sign of repentance, an attempt to receive remission of sins?

"Do you go to the mosque?" he asked Frederik.

"Sometimes I go to church with my wife and child. Usually on the holidays: Easter, Christmas, that sort," Frederik replied abruptly.

"And you, are you still as agnostic as you always were?" Frederik then asked him.

Karl shook his head affirmatively.

"In short, a genuine Albanian," Frederik commented. The smile on his face at that moment was like a stretching out of his hand for Karl to come closer on this night when their father's death had brought them together once again.

I remember some kids. One day two boys circled me behind our apartment house. In their hands they held stones. One of the kids, the bigger one, had a face full of freckles; the other was cross-eyed, as though an invisible hand had directed the pupil of one eye against the pupil of the other eye. Both kids had assumed a savage expression. For this the cross-eyed boy did not require any special effort since his eyes easily induced fear. Threatening me, they required me to give them the hat I was wearing. Otherwise they'd split my head open with their stones, two rocks they held with difficulty in their small, dusty fingers. The hat was white with a small green tiger on the side, embroidered by our mother before her fingers became paralyzed . . . I was panic stricken and began to wail mournfully. Karl then suddenly appeared with a long pole in hand, hooting like a knight engaged in solo combat. The two boys were bowled over. The rocks slipping out of their hands, they ran away in terror. The cross-eyed one fell down with only an "Ach" audible from his mouth. Then I saw him rise speedily and race away in fright.

I was six years old; Karl was eight. That day I felt protected. I have always liked feeling protected. I have always liked to think of Karl as my big brother . . .

When that time comes to mind I am overcome by nostalgia . . . I am extremely impressed that Karl never speaks of the past . . . perhaps because he does not see the past as a former home in which to gain some rest after returning, rest in which he can retrieve memory's pleasing warmth and repetition's security. Karl views the past like a dark, unknown island . . .

4

Karl, Frederik, and their aunt's two boys carried the coffin on their shoulders from the cemetery's central entrance to the open grave, next to the grave of Vali, Karl's and Frederik's mother. As was expected owing to the ritual of religious burials, the hodja commenced his prayers. Karl's thoughts while listening to the hodja's coarse voice were that he always felt ill at ease in the presence of clergymen no matter of what religion. This displeasure may have been one of the least of his father's influences upon him. Once upon a time an inveterate atheist who used to shout "God is dead!" his father had turned to religion a few years before he died, whereas Karl had remained unchangeably distrustful concerning God's presence in heaven and especially concerning His representatives on earth. The hodja finished his prayers by calling upon those present to repeat three times: "All of Omer's sins are forgiven; all of Omer's sins are forgiven; all of Omer's sins are forgiven."

When the wooden coffin began to be lowered into the grave's dark mouth, Karl heard Frederik's sobs and the tearful sounds of others. For a moment he felt that he had viewed this entire scene once before, somewhere, sometime. Surrounded by the grieving mourners, he felt benumbed, unable to weep, suddenly enwrapped by a sense of guilt resembling a hidden snake slithering in the bushes. He sensed it slinking inside him like a tangible creature ascending from his stomach to proceed across his lungs and reach his heart.

Frederik began in a broken voice to read a short funeral oration on behalf of the family. When he finished, he turned discreetly toward Karl and whispered in his ear, "Do you want to say two words?" Karl, attempting to hide his turmoil, shook his head slightly to indicate his refusal. "You be the first then to throw soil on the coffin," Frederik told him. "You'll need to throw three times; that's the custom." Karl, without speaking, bent down three times, filled his fists three times with soil, and threw the soil three times on the coffin.

• ■ •

A little after the funeral supper in their apartment's sitting room, without the presence of hired mourners or of male visitors in the other room, Karl asked himself if he had done well in deciding to remain another two weeks in Ters. During that time he would be alone with his brother Frederik in the home where they had grown up: an apartment of three bedrooms, a kitchen, two balconies, and two bathrooms, considered a great privilege during the communist period. He felt relieved when he thought that, besides the two of them, Frederik's wife and their twenty-year-old son would be there, whose presence he felt to be like the airbags installed in automobiles in case of a crash. He himself failed to understand the source of this fear of collision with his brother. However, he did sense that the fear was just as real as their father's death, as the old stone houses of Ters on the hill, and as the deformed apartment buildings of the new city all around them.

Frederik told Karl that he would sleep in their father's room, which Frederik's wife Majlinda had already prepared. It was formerly the children's room, where Karl and Frederik had slept when they were young. Since Frederik's marriage, it had become the father's room. Karl was flustered by the thought that he would sleep in the same bed in which the deceased father had slept until just a few days previously. But he did not say anything. In any case, he felt so exhausted that not even a trace of strength remained in him any longer to nourish his mind with images from the past or speculation concerning the present.

The three previous days he had not slept more than about five or six hours all told.

• ■ •

Now he slept deeply for 12 hours without dreams. When he awakened, he had a strange feeling for a few seconds: he seemed to be in mid-ocean in an abandoned rowboat. Finding himself in the middle of nowhere bothered him; after all, he was in his father's former bedroom, in his own former childhood bedroom, in his life's most familiar space. His eyes wandered slowly over the photos and portraits hanging on the room's walls. There was a picture of his paternal grandfather, whom Karl had never known. He had heard again and again from his father the story of this grandfather who disappeared during the period of German occupation — about how, accused of harboring Jews, he was arrested by a German patrol in front of the eyes of his son and wife. Karl's father was then five years old, his grandfather thirty. All traces of him vanished after the arrest. They never learned what happened or where the Germans had deported him. Karl's father believed that they had smothered him together with Jews in the gas chambers of Auschwitz. In the photo on the wall this paternal grandfather must have been around 20 years old. Wearing small, round, black-framed, myopic eyeglasses, he resembled a Parisian-style portrait of the 1930s.

Next to this portrait of Karl's vanished grandfather was one of his own father when very young, the marks of adolescence still upon his face, a leaden-gray sky above his head. He was posing in front of Lenin's Mausoleum in Moscow sporting his customary mien: that of someone who hated jokes.

Running through Karl's mind again was the moment he had first set eyes upon his deceased father. He hesitated a bit before telling Frederik that he wished to remain alone with the dead body for five minutes. The women around the coffin silently left the room as soon as they heard Karl's wish. On the way out they gave him a quick look — half in curiosity, half in fear — as though Karl had decided to descend into the House of the Dead.

Remaining alone with the coffin, Karl gently moved the black lid aside and saw the deceased covered with flowers from the feet to high up on the chest, dressed in a black suit and white shirt. The son, reaching out, rested his hand upon his father's brow. A tempestuous wave of sorrow flooded him. He had been feeling like a collector of sorrows for a long time. Like someone else collecting butterflies or postcards, Karl collected sorrows.

• ■ •

He had the same feeling when viewing his dead mother. Life having abandoned someone, how masklike that person's face becomes! The dead father's features resembled an aged, serene mask while those of the dead mother were like the mask of someone who had departed her life lacking sufficient time to express a huge complaint. She had left nothing but a short note: "Frederik and Karl, forgive me for what I am doing. I love you very much. V," at the end of which was a heart, hastily drawn by her paralyzed fingers . . . Each day their mother had lost additional control of her mind and body. With her limbs deforming, her nervous system deadening, her mind fading away, every day that passed was excised from her world. The hospital psychiatrist revealed that she had been tormented for a long time with thoughts of suicide. The autopsy showed that she had taken a dose of cyanide, one of the most lethal poisons. It was never discovered how this had fallen into her hands. She had remained exemplarily mysterious even in this most self-destructive act of hers. Karl had spent days and entire weeks hoping that he would find a note hidden somewhere in her clothing or personal effects, written exclusively for him before her fatal act. He did not abandon this vain hope even now that he had returned for his father's funeral.

• ■ •

The moment he saw his mother in the morgue, Karl felt that an umbilical cord linking him with life's center of gravity had been brutally severed; he resembled a boat tied to the pier when a hurricane snaps its cables, leaving it adrift in an enraged sea.

Recently he had been asking himself whether he had strayed from one place to another as a migrant, unconsciously hoping that he would again find that displaced center of the world, that umbilical cord which had been violently cut at some point. After so many years, he was not in a position to say if he had found it. As for his brother, Frederik had always remained loyal to their father's philosophy — namely, "Even the worst of fatherlands is better than any foreign place."

Karl had lived beneath different skies, had spoken and written foreign languages, had loved women of different ethnicities. Frederik had lived in the same town where he was born, in the same apartment house, on the same floor, in the same apartment, fulfilling in this way the ideal of generations continuing without a gap — something that, according to their father, grants to human beings a happy existence and strong identity.

• ■ •

The last time Karl had seen his father alive was five years earlier, a few weeks before he left for America. He was surprised how rapidly this man had aged who had always appeared strong and energetic, one of those who manage to hide their years beneath adroit locomotion and a well-maintained skin. But his skin was then visibly worn and his bodily motion suddenly slower. Mental alertness was also beginning to decline.

This last meeting was perhaps the most difficult. They were eating their evening meal in the dining room when his father asked Karl if he intended to create a family. With an embarrassed smile, Karl responded that one day that too would happen. Afterwards, eager to break the silence that rested on the table like an invisible block of ice, Karl revealed that he was preparing to leave Greece so that he could migrate to America. He endeavored to present this new place of settlement as something quite ordinary, a decision that simply would change his life for the better. He did not report the chance meeting with Klodi in Athens, the rejection of his application for Greek citizenship, the life-threatening messages he had been receiving for many months, or the fact that he had ended in the hospital covered with blood after being savagely beaten. He feared that if he reported all of this, his father would have stated once again in his well-known sarcastic manner: "I have already told you this: Even the worst fatherland is better than any foreign place."

Karl was surprised that his father remained silent when he heard about this next emigration — to America this time. Only when he was preparing to rise from table was he suddenly asked: "Aren't you tired, Karl, of passing your whole life speaking other people's languages?" Karl felt as though someone had removed his clothing with a magical gesture and rendered him naked. His father's face emitted a dark sorrow. Karl stared at the eyes but this time saw no sign of the customary ironic glance. Feeling that words were no longer left to him, he did not speak.

"Will we ever see each other again?" his father asked the following day when they were saying goodbye. In his voice, Karl discerned something like supplication, the first time he had ever detected anything of that sort. "Naturally we'll get together again," he replied — another promise that he never kept, as when he had said that he would return in six months. Regarding these unkept promises, Karl attempted to find consolation in an unforeseen journey or in the peculiar psychology of refugees, who always promise to return when in the end most of them never do. For Karl, the myth of Odysseus, who goes back to Ithaca after exhausting travel, was nothing but a lovely fairy tale with no relevance whatsoever to the reality of any contemporary Odysseus, whose present-day incarnations abandon their Ithacas, as he does, and leave for the unknown, playing heads or tails with their luck, hunting for a dream or a delusion, hoping that wherever they go they will recreate themselves again out of nothing. In the last analysis, Karl thought, isn't the ancient Odysseus one of the most contradictory heroes of human history?

I am saddened by the thought that Karl never really cared for our family. Take his relationship with our mother, for example. He always behaved as though Mother belonged solely to him. As for me and our father, Karl's aim was to depart as far as possible from us, as though away from us he would find whatever he was seeking . . . Sometimes I have the impression that Karl departed solely to punish Father. At other times I fear that he himself does not know why he went away and what exactly he has been seeking. Father used to say, "Karl misspends his intelligence on delusions." Surely I, too, have delusions, but they do not become so self-destructive when you live among your own people. When you cut the roots that attach you to your family, your city, your language, when you scatter your body and soul everywhere like so many orphans, as Karl has done, then the delusions, resembling snow on a mountainside, become a drift that sooner or later falls on you as an avalanche to crush you . . .

•5•

What would he do in Ters for the next two weeks? His former acquaintances were not there any longer, most having settled in Tirana or emigrated to other countries. In his relationship with his brother Frederik he had long ago become cold and aloof. Karl's 27 years of geographic distance from Ters, except for brief visits of only a few days each, had raised an insurmountable wall between them.

Despite all that, Karl felt this time that his return was somehow different, that in some way it reached beyond his father's death and burial. Looking through the window of their former childhood room, he observed the endless blue dome of Ters's sky. Into his mind came the words of Vexhi, the locally well-known translator who was nicknamed Tower of Babel by the Tersians and was perpetually condemned to internal banishment within the city: "The heart becomes intoxicated when it sees this gorgeous sky above people's heads. The heart becomes mournful when it sees the frightened, repudiated people below."

Seeing Ters's bright vault on that winter morning, Karl realized that before emigrating to America he had spent his entire life beneath sunny skies. Living the last five years in Boston with Klodi, his greatest cultural shock was the fact that the word "snow" (marginal until then) and all its derivatives — "snowstorm warning," "snow blower," "snowplow," "winter boots," "winter jackets," "thermal T-shirts," "thermal underwear," "parka," "blizzard," "black ice" — had become one of his vocabulary's basic items.

Klodi attempted in every way to teach Karl how to accept snow and become reconciled to wintertime and its melancholy. On Sundays, when they enjoyed the day off, they remained stretched out in bed until late, conversing or caressing each other beneath the sound of melodies by Debussy. Klodi would whisper then in his ear: "Winter is the most beautiful season for those whose heart is warm." Sometimes, when the snow invaded the city's every corner and frost made a person's relation with nature resemble an undeclared duel, they both vowed that perhaps (perhaps!) they would someday go to live in California or even Italy — places at any rate with plentiful sunshine. Klodi knew inwardly, however, that something like that was never going to happen. Accustomed to the chilliness of both residents and climate, she endeavored to become reconciled to Boston. To abandon this city struck her now as so difficult, almost impossible any longer. She hoped that her two children as well, when they finished university, would continue to live in Boston or somewhere nearby. She hoped that Karl would grow used to it, get to know it, accept it, would even come to love this city, just as she had learned to accept and love it. For Klodi, love of cities and people was almost identical. What else was love, she wondered, except that sentiment of feeling at last reconciled to the finitude of your existence and the infinitude of the universe whenever you find yourself near the location and the human being that you covet?

• ■ •

Karl knew why his visit to Ters was different this time: It was the question of where he would be buried after he died. Would it be in the place of death or here in his birthplace, in this strange disfigured city beneath a warm, all-blue sky? The dilemma had penetrated his mind for the first time a few months after he emigrated from Greece to America, having invaded him like an uncalled-for visitor on the day he entered Mount Auburn Cemetery, one of the most famous burial parklands in greater Boston, where people go more to enjoy a picnic than to ponder the meaning of life and death. The idea to visit the cemetery was not his; Klodi had convinced him to accompany her one autumn day when nature in New England was wearing its most attractive shawl, that of dying leaves.

Where would he wish to be buried when he died? Initially he tried to conclude that this suddenly devised question was senseless. He had just turned 45 and had recently arrived in America, he told himself. He still had lots of time in front of him before the necrophobic cares of aging commenced. All in all, he was convinced that a citizen of the world as he was should not torment himself with such dilemmas. Wasn't he the one who, full of melancholy passion, had recited one day to Klodi Joseph Brodsky's verse: "Thank God that I have been left on the earth without a fatherland"? Karl belonged to the category of those who had abandoned and lost not just one fatherland but two: Albania and Greece.

Since the day his mother had committed suicide, thoughts of death were always present in Karl's mind. He might die at any moment; his life and the lives of other known or unknown people around him were, by virtue of either some paradoxical event or some terrifying means, entirely fragile. On the other hand, his dilemma concerning where he would be buried after his death was something new and different, something that previously had never preoccupied him. As the days, weeks, and months passed by, the more he tried to ignore this dilemma, all the more did the concern pursue him.

Only when he gained American citizenship, swearing eternal faith to the Constitution of the United States together with a mass of individuals from every possible corner of the world, had the troubling thought of his corpse's posthumous residence somehow faded away. Yet days occurred when that thought returned with a persistence almost violent, as happens with the ghosts of familiar individuals who visit us in our sleep. Karl realized that something like this was perhaps caused by the fact that, when a person approaches the age of 50, fear of death becomes a permanent inhabitant of his mind. Socrates in ancient Athens must have been approximately 50 when he said that philosophy is above all a study of death. Yet even this speculation had failed to repulse Karl's idée fixe. Now that he was back in Ters for his father's funeral, it had returned again torrentially, like a violent visitor who threatens not to leave the home he has invaded unless given whatever he demands.

Something else making Karl underrate me is the fact that he considers me . . . (how to say it?) . . . a "hick" because I never burned with a desire to abandon Ters . . . Even when everyone was leaving on the double, I kept saying to myself: "This is your city, your fate." . . . I have identified my destiny with the destiny of Ters. I know every centimeter of this city just as I know every centimeter of my body . . . And each time I go down to the morgue and see people's lifeless bodies I understand why I never deserted Ters, never became a wandering migrant like Karl. My homeland is where my deceased are found. The further away I go from them, the more reduced becomes my strength, my life, my identity.

6

"Aren't you tired, Karl, of passing your whole life speaking other people's languages?" his father had asked him the last time they saw each other, as Karl was preparing to leave Greece for America in a new migration. The truth was that Karl exhibited a lifelong passionate love for the sound of other peoples' tongues, this being perhaps an innate talent for foreign languages, something that later became a way of life.

He was approximately five years old when he had learned his first words of Russian from his father and of French from his mother — the foreign languages they spoke. "We want to raise our son a polyglot," they said, and they glowed with pride when they observed Karl showing a juggler's dexterity in his play with foreign words. The parents had ventured the same with Frederik, but without the same success. When encircled by foreign words, Frederik was found to be in disarray, fallen into a profound silence. The pediatrician they consulted recommended that the parents delay their aspiration to raise two polyglot children until later. Frederik's memory, said the physician, suffered something like a short circuit and chose silence in self-defense. "With the other son we did not have a similar problem," father sighed. "Children are not born with the same talents, comrade Omer," replied the pediatrician.

Subsequently, with monkish perseverance and dedication, using passé dictionaries and outmoded grammar books with torn pages, Karl taught himself Italian, Spanish, and English. Foreign words were converted little by little into a magic carpet upon which his thoughts enabled him to travel to places — Saint Petersburg, Paris, Rome, Barcelona, London — where these words were spoken. The sounds and colors of the cities that Karl visited in his imagination were different from the sounds and murky colors of Ters. Nevertheless, the more he devoted himself to the languages of others, amassing foreign words like a raving collector, the more did his father's glance radiate misgiving while his mother's radiated admiration.

Father was enthusiastic at the start regarding his son's rare gift for foreign languages. Yet when Karl began to bring home, besides foreign words, excerpts, illustrations, and forbidden songs that he secretly captured from their German Grundig radio or by reading condemned books among those on the regime's endless blacklist, Father felt as though the earth beneath his feet were slipping away. He had hoped that when Karl matured he would utilize all of his talents "for the good of the nation and the Party" (as Father always said in his solemn, pompous style). He hoped that Karl would translate the work of Enver H., the Leader, into other languages. Father himself had produced translations of the writings of Lenin and Stalin from Russian into Albanian, the published volumes of which with their ornate covers were visible in a conspicuous location in the family's home library. But it appears that the situation with Karl had taken an unexpected turn. Father followed with indignant consternation Karl's transformation into a smuggler of images and fragments from another world, a forbidden one that Father considered dangerous, hostile, menacing . . .

• ▪ •

Tiranovskaja biblioteka — that is how Karl had once called the large library that occupied most of their apartment's hallway. Father looked after the library with religious devotion. Every weekend he dusted the books, enriched them with new items, tidied them by placing them in order like parading soldiers. Occasionally it chanced that he would reduce and impoverish the library, removing books that the Party had classified as undesirable. (This happened, for example, with the books of Mao Zedong, which had vanished from the library the same day that China, Albania's closest friend, had suddenly been proclaimed a hostile country.)

Tiranovskaja biblioteka was a pun in Russian that meant "library of Tirana" but also "library of the Tyrant." Father was leafing through a book at the moment he heard Karl pronounce those words behind his back: Tiranovskaja biblioteka. The day had just begun to grow dark when through the sitting-room window, which always remained open during the summer, came the city's uproar. All day long the inhabitants of Ters sheltered themselves from the hot sun beneath the rooftops of their homes but as soon as sunset commenced they poured out toward Ters's Great Square, endeavoring to find much desired shade beneath the tall poplars circling it.

Father, turning his head, saw Karl's mocking expression. He then launched his hand like a stone from the library shelf to Karl's face. Everything happened speedily, as in a bad dream. Karl was not aware of how he had collapsed with a thud onto the floor, astonished and intimidated. Frederik was not then present. Mother howled from the armchair in the sitting room and extended her deformed hands in Karl's direction. He, lying on the floor bewildered and afraid, did not dare to move. Father stood over him breathing with difficulty as though that very moment he were supporting Ters's sky on his shoulders. Pointing at Karl with his index finger like a pistol he uttered, "If you say that again I'll kill you!" He then rushed out of the apartment slamming the door behind him. Karl momentarily imagined he had emerged from his body and was observing it from a distance as though it belonged to some unknown individual. In his mouth he tasted blood flowing from his nose. The Great Square's uproar entering through the window reached his ears like the inarticulate jabbering of a delirious multitude.

This episode of paternal violence would remain glued to Karl's memory like a leech to human skin. He would view the scene again and again while asleep or awake. It was not his blue-black nose from the blow, or the taste of blood on his palate, or the awareness that he and his body had become momentarily foreign to each other. It was his father's gaze the moment he uttered, "I'll kill you" — the fanatic's gaze from which you could neither hide nor escape: as cold as ice, as shiny as the sharp blade of the sharpest knife, as inexorable as a disease that can never be cured.

Karl was destined to encounter another fanatic's gaze many years afterwards, many miles away from Ters, beneath another sky, surrounded by the foreign words of another language. He would encounter it on a springtime evening in Athens, one of those nights where, despite pollution, the city's atmosphere is as light and gentle as a caress, so much so that you feel like shedding your clothes and rambling naked through the streets, happy simply and exclusively because you exist. On such a night, Karl would again see the same gaze as his father's in Ters, the same dark glitter in the eyes, the same hate-swollen lips that pronounced the same threat, this time in Greek: "I'll kill you!"

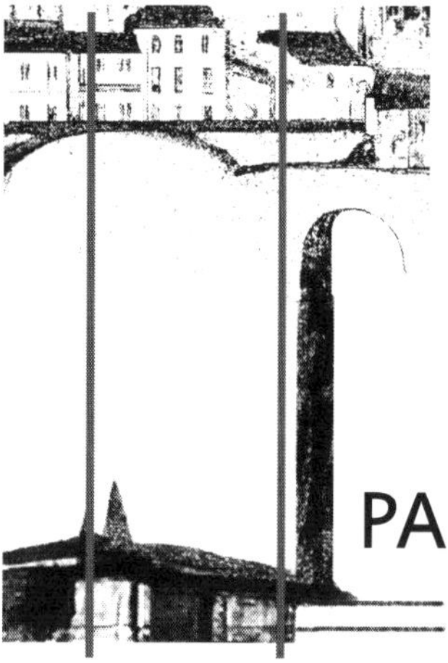

PART 2

• 1 •

Tirana's tumult began a few weeks after the suicide of Karl's mother. Anti-regime slogans such as "Ceauşescu Awaits You in Hell" suddenly appeared next to the regime's faded, outdated slogans on apartment house façades such as "WATER SLEEPS, THE ENEMY DOES NOT." At first the anti-regime ones vanished at the drop of a hat; a few weeks later, however, they began to remain untouched right next to the pro-regime slogans, like two mutually spiteful roommates. People rubbed their eyes with wonder and disbelief as they enjoyed the anti-regime slogans that had survived for entire days — until it became known that these had not been covered over owing to a lack of whitewash. Voices in the cafés then grew louder and more courageous, declaring that a regime lacking whitewash was in fact already kaput. However, when several of the patrons fell victim to the well-trained ears of stool pigeons and paid for their pleasure with arrest and fierce beatings in the dungeons of the secret police, they whispered fearfully in voices once again hushed, "Whitewash lacking but informers still plentiful, fuck their mothers!"

Long ago Karl's family had split into two camps, Mother and Karl on one side, Father and Frederik on the other. Neither Mother nor Karl hid their scorn for the regime. These two were the "xenomaniacs," as Father scornfully named them. Father and Frederik had baptized each other as "patriots." Now that the regime was faltering, they declared themselves in favor of deliberate, careful changes. "Let us fix what is wrong and retain the many things that are right," Father kept irritably repeating.

Having become increasingly cantankerous after his wife's death, he never discussed this harrowing event in front of his boys. He had apparently convinced himself that she died from a heart attack. At the funeral he looked overwhelmed but did not weep. Karl often thought that perhaps his father bore a grudge against his wife owing to this decision of hers to put an end to her life. Nor was it fortuitous that fanatic communists considered suicide one of the most despicable acts, being in their eyes the ultimate expression of insubordination and self-determination. But perhaps he felt betrayed by his wife because in her last words before the fatal act she had not made even the slightest reference to him.

• ▪ •

The Humanities Department at the university had been converted into a center of student rebellion against the regime. But Karl, always preferring solitude, did not become involved with any of the coordinating committees for the demonstrations. After his mother's suicide, he became even more self-enclosed. In addition, as the son of a communist who still swore by the Party's "ideals" and had filled his home with portraits of the dictator, these days Karl was overcome with pangs of guilt more than ever before. He was therefore surprised when he realized that many of those chairing the committees, having discovered the charm of disobedience, were the regime's pampered children. Clearly they were not tormented by feelings of guilt or shame.

At bottom they were rebelling not against their fathers but were simply taking care to secure an advantageous position in the new period whenever the former regime was replaced by a new one, no matter what its form or name.

• ■ •

The only time that Karl participated in a demonstration was six months after his mother's death, the day when the giant statue of Enver H. came down — February 20, 1991. It was a cold Wednesday, the sky above Tirana covered with large, thick clouds that resembled eyes swollen from lack of sleep. The special police forces, which had occupied Tirana's central square and had formed a living wall around the dictator's statue, kept looking at these bloated black eyes in the sky, praying for rain — their only hope for dispersing the crowd.

Instead of rain, however, what began to fall was an endless hailstorm of stones that the infuriated crowd launched to attack the police, who replied with rubber bullets, a baton charge, and trained, large-bodied sheepdogs that seemed to bury their teeth impetuously in the demonstrators' flesh. They, the dogs, appeared the most resolute to protect the dictator's statue. As for the police, they apparently were at their wits' end, like people who have lost their orientation and self-confidence, perhaps because they failed to know under whose command they would be serving when they awoke the next morning — under those defending the statue or those wishing to pull it down. They resembled windmills struggling to understand in which direction the gusts of history were blowing. As for the dogs, however, not suffering from such dilemmas, they remained ever faithful to the mission for which they had been trained by human beings.

● ■ ●

Karl, hidden behind the Et'hem Bey Mosque, kept watching the conflict between demonstrators and police plus sinister sheepdogs. After 23 years of forbidden religion, the mosque had recently begun to offer services again. The faithful were emerging after midday prayers at the very moment when the clash around the dictator's statue in the middle of Tirana's central square had taken the form of a battle between life and death. Some of the Muslim faithful, swept away by enthusiasm, ran toward the crowded demonstrators and hid in their midst like drops of water in an angry sea. The remainder, huddled like Karl behind the mosque's wall, having prayed inside to Allah privately for various benefits, now begged Him collectively to help the crowd pull down the tyrant's statue. A little removed from the others, an elderly woman crossed herself and prayed to Jesus to rescue human beings from bloodshed by descending to earth. The demonstrators, bleeding now from rubber bullets, genuine bullets, and sheepdogs' teeth, after plundering the pavement and hurling its cobbles at the statue's defenders, had managed toward early afternoon to break the policemen's barricade.

At that moment, Karl ran toward the crowd.

● ■ ●

Neither the sheepdogs' hungry teeth, the policemen's baton charge, the heartbreaking cries of the demonstrators — "O mother, mother, I'm dying!" — nor the image of a young blood-covered girl stretched on the ground could halt Karl any longer. He had been transformed into a single drop within this ocean of human beings who possessed one purpose only: to pull down the dictator's statue.

After about half an hour, when he found himself in front of the statue's bronze feet surrounded by thousands of mouths shouting as though proclaiming the Messiah's return, Karl felt that his body had acquired magical qualities, making him invincible, imperishable, invulnerable. His hands then took hold of a thick rope tied around the statue's waist. Together with the others, howling like a galley slave, he began to haul on the rope with all his strength. When the dictator's statue started to budge, the surrounding crowd began to sling out curses in their hoarse voices: "Down with the son of a fucking mother" (because mothers are involved even when dictators are involved; no one ever cursed a dictator's father).

The huge statue moved slightly at first like a hog that, realizing it was being taken for slaughter, digs its hoofs into the ground with all the pigheadedness bequeathed it by the survival instinct. Afterwards the entire monument shook as though stricken with epilepsy. The moment it began tipping toward the ground, small raindrops began to fall from the sky. A few years later, Karl would write in his journal, "I have never again seen the Albanians so insane with joy as at that moment. I have often seen them insane with misery, or simply insane without the slightest cause . . ."

• ▪ •

The demonstrators wore murky dull-colored clothing; the dictator wore an enormous, luxurious overcoat of bronze. When the statue lay on the ground like a corpse devoid of any hope for resurrection, the demonstrators began to strike it with their bare fists, to kick it with feet exhausted from fatigue, to spit on it with mouths parched with thirst yet nevertheless frothing with mixed ecstasy and hate. The dictator at that point was nothing more than a lifeless shell at the mercy of his infuriated former slaves.

After 20 minutes of collective delirium, some of the crowd climbed up onto the statue. They covered the cadaver's every inch as though they had boarded a magical boat, perhaps the most fun-loving hearse ever seen in human history. Karl, too, clambered up onto the dictator. The moment he found a foothold he began to sob convulsively. He saw the enraptured masses through tear-flooded eyes and felt they were dancing. How very much he wished that his mother had experienced this moment, that they had celebrated the monster's fall together. While father and Frederik hung their heads in bitterness and defeat, he and she would have jointly shouted, "Free at last!"

• ▪ •

The demonstrators who had not managed to scale the bronze carcass tied ropes around the dictator's statue and began to drag it through Tirana's streets, heading for the university campus, where the ceremonial ritual of dismemberment would be performed. Both those who were pulling and those who had mounted the corpse were laughing, weeping, cursing, jeering, embracing each other, waving in the air their tiny palms that seemed so full, as though they had conquered the sky.

When they reached their destination, they began to dismember the corpse with zeal and haste, as though fearing the body would come to life if they delayed. Karl, stepping off the statue, quickly took his place in the "sledgehammer queue," as it was called. This was a long line of young university students each of whom passed to the next a sledgehammer with which that individual maniacally struck the dethroned dictator. When the sledgehammer finally reached Karl's hands, he began mercilessly, incessantly, to strike the bronze head until he was breathless. The horribly mutilated head was the first to break away, together with a part of the statue's chest. A few of the demonstrators attempted without success to extract the eyes. Next they pulled away the right hand, which was holding the luxurious overcoat, after that the right foot, finally the right thigh. The surrounding crowd kept watching the dismemberment process. Time and space had been overwhelmed by obscene curses against the dictator, by sobbing, and by cheering happiness.

● ■ ●

When Karl began to distance himself from the statue and to head for the students' center at about four o'clock in the morning, the dismemberment of the bronze corpse had been mostly completed. Surrounding the remains were young men and women drinking ample amounts of raki and wine while loving couples embraced on top of what was still intact after the dismemberment. Others were dancing to tunes of Cyndi Lauper and Prince. Occasionally some of the youngsters, blinded from drink, unable to decide who would commandeer the dictator's fingers and who his toes, exchanged punches. It never entered Karl's mind to help himself to some part of the dismembered statue as a souvenir. All he wanted at that moment was to return to his room and fall asleep. He felt that he had swum the Adriatic Sea. Beginning to walk slowly, he realized that he had lost his left shoe in the confusion. Dizzily, he searched for it . . .

● ■ ●

"Could you be looking for your shoe?" he heard a female voice ask behind his back. Turning his head, he tried to discern the person's face in the semi-darkness. An unknown girl was holding a bottle of beer in one hand and a black shoe in the other. Taking two or three steps toward him, she offered the shoe.

Karl remained a few seconds with the shoe in hand as though dazed.

"Yes, it's my shoe," he murmured. "Where did you find it?"

"I am Klodi," the unknown girl declared instead of replying. She offered her hand to him.

"Karl," he said.

"Karl like Karl Marx?" she asked, laughing.

"Yes, Karl like Karl Marx," he answered somewhat hesitatingly.

"You're joking! Ha ha! Just imagine, Karl Marx with a sledgehammer smashing the head of one of his followers," she said, her body jiggling from laughter again. (Many years later, in entirely different circumstances, Klodi would learn that Karl owed his name to the dictator's "magnanimity.")

"University student?" Karl asked to change the subject.

"No, comrade Marx. Class war, you see, which means a bad CV. No rights for us, no studies," answered the unknown girl downing yet another sip from her beer bottle. Her eyes turned suddenly cold.

"Can I drink a sip?" Karl then asked.

"Of course! From what I know, you Germans drink a lot," she said, offering the bottle to him.

Karl realized that the unknown girl was dizzy from alcohol.

"I study French literature," said Karl.

"Vive la Révolution alors!" she replied, assuming a pompous pose.

The two of them began an aimless walk. With a nod, Karl indicated a bench to her at the side of the road. They sat down without conversing, wrapped in darkness. Reaching their ears came the sound of yelling and music around the dismembered statue. About 50 yards from the bench, in the gloom, an embracing couple was passionately kissing and caressing with frequent sensuous moans.

"I read somewhere that revolutions are accompanied by sexual orgies," she said with a bantering laugh.

Karl raised his eyes toward heaven instead of answering.

"You must be the only male in Albania who does not behave like a famished pig when he meets a half-intoxicated female," said Klodi. Then, as though worried about what she had said, she too raised her eyes toward heaven.

"It's going to rain. Twenty years from now the communists will affirm that nature wept on the day the Leader's statue fell," she said.

Karl grasped her arm gently and pulled her toward him. He felt his heart beating strongly from agitation and fear of rejection. She did not resist. Their faces approached until one touched the other in the half-darkness. He sensed beer-smell on her breath. Their lips joined.

Suddenly she withdrew, breathing deeply.

"Your kiss betrays a rich experience with women, Mr. Marx," said Klodi as she downed still another sip from the bottle.

"I'd like very much for us to sleep together tonight," said Karl, his voice trembling.

She looked into his eyes, touched his lips gently with her fingers and smiled when Karl kissed her hands with closed eyes.

"Unfortunately we're out of luck. Impediments that nature preserves for women, you understand . . .," she said, fluttering her eyes.

Karl said nothing.

"Let me ask you something, Mr. Marx. Do you want us to talk again tomorrow?" she inquired, once again in her playful style.

"Yes," said Karl, holding her hand in his.

"Tomorrow, then, at 12:30 in Fine Arts," said

Klodi, rising. Karl rose in turn. Together they began to descend the slope away from the university campus and toward her house. They walked without speaking, each looking at the other and smiling, as though they wished to confirm that the other was real and not something invented by the fantasy of that insane night. When they reached Skanderbeg Square at the break of dawn, they saw the empty base of the dictator's statue surrounded by soldiers and tanks. Policemen and soldiers stood silently motionless. They resembled waxwork images from Madame Tussaud's.

"What exactly are they guarding now?" whispered Klodi.

"They themselves don't know any longer," said Karl.

They continued to walk hand in hand as though that moment did not exist, nor did the police, the tanks, the black sheepdogs. Klodi's home was near city center in a three-story apartment house behind the Tirana Tower. She pointed to her apartment's window on the third floor. The light was still on.

"It's daylight, but my mother is still waiting for me," she said.

"Tomorrow noon," said Karl, coming close to kiss her.

"Isn't life a strange, crazy show, Mr. Marx?" whispered Klodi.

"Won't you tell me where you found my shoe?" Karl asked her.

"I'll tell you tomorrow," she replied.

Her voice was happy.

He kissed her gently on the neck and stood in front of the apartment house door until Klodi disappeared on the staircase like a shadow.

• ■ •

When Karl awoke later that morning, he no longer sensed the frenzied joy of the preceding day. His eyes felt heavy; an abysmal vacancy in his breast was dragging him to its bottom. His hands were swollen from yesterday's blows with the sledgehammer. Jumping out of bed, worried lest the time be late, he looked at the clock and found that he still had an hour before his rendezvous with Klodi. Dressing speedily, he left his room.

Prevailing outdoors was a silence charged with both hope and fear. The few people who walked the streets at that hour turned their heads neither to left nor right lest their motion provoke some outbreak. Speechless policemen and soldiers stood motionless next to the sports arena Qemal Stafa and around the Italian and French embassies. A little further down, a living wall of police and soldiers armed to the teeth had surrounded the Bloc, the neighborhood that housed members of the Politburo. The only people circulating without worry were two Gypsies around the School of Fine Arts who were inviting passersby to display their palms and thereby learn what was bound to happen to them in the future.

• ■ •

Karl waited in front of the School of Fine Arts for about two hours. Klodi did not appear. Disheartened and worried, he decided to look for her in the apartment house where they had said goodbye the previous night. He climbed its stairs hesitatingly and on the second floor encountered an elderly woman who was dragging her steps with difficulty. Karl offered a hand to help her; she thanked him. He asked if she knew a young woman on the third floor named Klodi.

"Yes, Klodi, that pretty girl, Hanna's daughter," said the old woman. "Mother and daughter left this morning for Israel."

"Israel?" Karl repeated, perplexed.

"Yes, the Israeli Embassy has gathered up all those skinflints. At least they escaped," said the aged woman, taking out her keys to open her apartment door.

• ■ •

The disappearance of Klodi, who had entered Karl's life like a momentary dream, converted into a mania his desire to leave Albania. Everyone else seemed overcome by the same craving. Like prisoners craving to abandon their cells or murderers the sites of their crimes, Albanians yearned to desert their country as soon as possible after their half century of absolute isolation from the world.

Karl passed his final months of university lectures in a condition of impatience and melancholy. The campus, where a few weeks earlier he had dismembered the dictator's statue, now seemed like both a desert and a jungle. Students appeared with decreasing frequency not only on campus but even inside the lecture halls, since harassment and rape had reached epidemic proportions. The police force, everywhere evident before the dictatorship's fall, had now totally disappeared. Professors as well had vanished out of the blue. No one discovered where they had gone, but news would come after a few days that some had emigrated to Europe, others to the United States, Canada, Australia, wherever they could. Those faithful to the regime, or nostalgic for it, smirked at the sight of the chaos that had replaced dictatorship. Smugly patting their tummies and well-shaven chins, they asseverated, "Enjoy democracy and freedom!"

Father was among those who repeated this refrain with malicious enjoyment. Karl had attempted to avoid any clash with him after his mother's suicide; he was simply waiting to receive his diploma, which he kept thinking might be useful wherever he might be. On that day he would escape his father, heading as far away from him as his feet and imagination could bring him. This inhuman dictatorship, he whispered to himself, is what has driven people to view their nation as though stricken by a plague.

Humanity is unfinished, chaotic. Its heart and mind possess boundaries and limits just as every house has its doorstep. These limits and boundaries are called identity, family, ethnicity, roots. Human nature has made it this way: to love first and foremost the portion of humanity to which one belongs, especially those who possess the same blood, speak the same language, have the same skin color, share the same fate, are soaked by the same rain and sea, are shaken by the same earthquake, partake of the same dreams and fears.

I remember when one day Father spoke to us about the meaning of family, ethnicity, and roots. But Karl said, "People are not trees, to have roots. People have feet and dreams. They want to travel, but all of you have shut them up as though in a cage, like animals." What followed was one of the fierce arguments that occurred between Karl and Father. Every time they quarreled, something broke inside me . . .

I am not like Karl. I believe that people have roots. Thanks to these, we feel closer to siblings than to cousins, closer to neighbors than to people we do not know, closer to our own language than to other peoples' languages, closer to our fatherland than to other peoples' fatherlands . . .

• 2 •

1991.
The final week of October.

Karl entered Greece at the Kakavia/Kakavijë crossing with a fake visa made for a price by Tirana's most celebrated counterfeiter, Goni son of Fatime. (Six months after Karl crossed the border, Goni son of Fatime was found butchered in his home, his unusually large palms like two oars floating in a blood-filled lake together with hundreds of passport stamps from all the recognized nations of the European Union.)

"It's lucky you have a Christian name. That eases my work with the Greeks," Goni son of Fatime told him before placing him in the care of a smuggler who accompanied Karl as far as No Man's Land at the Greek-Albanian border.

"When the Greek police ask you your name, scratch your head with the left hand," the smuggler told him, belching. He was a fat man about 40 years old. "Don't forget to scratch with the left hand, not the right," he repeated this time with urgency as he left Karl in No Man's Land. Shaking his head affirmatively, Karl joined the crowd of Albanians who were there, some for hours, most for days. At the last minute before they separated, the smuggler came closer to Karl, just a breath away, and it seemed to Karl that the man's entire being was emitting the smell of yogurt pie.

That was the only smell he stored in his memory from that day. Everything else imprinted on his mind consisted of colors, shapes, dimensions, or sounds — the blue color of the enormous brand-new Greek flag nailed to the Greek customs house, its shadow so large that it covered No Man's Land, versus the faded red of the Albanian flag (like a person dying from a severe illness), which seemed to have been placed so that it could wave above the Albanian customs house as a form of punishment; the black and ashen-gray clothes of the Albanians waiting in front of the Greek frontier, hoping to leave Albania behind them and to cross to the other side with or without a visa, with a fake or a genuine passport.

These totally silent Albanians, like starving men fixing their eyes on a plateful of food, had fixed their eyes on the Greek border and police. The gaze of the elderly resembled the gaze of frightened children, the gaze of the children that of the elderly. They were all waiting anxiously for a sign to come from the other side that would forever change their lives. But nothing was heard from the Greek side for hours on end except the yelping of a dog.

Karl waited there for 20 hours or more (he did not remember exactly how many). During that endless delay he did remember that he wanted to urinate all the time. But urination in No Man's Land was permitted only once in the twenty-four-hour period and then only after nightfall, in accord with regulations posted by the Greek border guards. This excruciating urination procedure, illuminated by a large searchlight that shone exclusively there, occurred on a mass basis behind a half-crumbled wall that stank of decaying dog cadavers.

He also remembered a skinny priest with a long beard who suddenly appeared unannounced at dawn on the Greek border and crossed himself thrice, aiming at the crowd in No Man's Land. When the Albanians witnessed the priest crossing himself for them, they began to rub eyes heavy with sleeplessness to be sure they had not gone cuckoo. As for Karl, he remembered that when the priest disappeared, indeed at the very moment of his disappearance, somebody nearby shared with him a slice of bread with feta cheese and small black olives.

Afterwards, as though by magic, he found himself on the border's opposite side. Albanians who made it to this other side were classified as Lucky Ones, a category that now included Karl thanks to Goni son of Fatime's fake visa and the scratch of his head with the left hand. From his border crossing he remembered a Greek policeman's eyes. They resembled those of an overfed cat.

• ■ •

The journey lasted eight hours. The bus in which Karl traveled was filled with Lucky Ones. During the entire route the passengers remained either silent or they conversed with gestures, like conspirators, as though they feared that if Albanian words were overheard the bus's motor would die and the border crossing be vitiated. Karl was traveling to Athens with the thought of remaining there for several weeks and then continuing his journey elsewhere: to Italy, France, England, perhaps Spain — one of the countries where he spoke the language. He did not possess a single word of Greek. Furthermore, Greece itself was entirely unknown to him and failed to tease his curiosity.

Like all the other passengers in the bus, he knew where he was leaving but had no idea about where he was going. In their minds they were all carrying a magical world map that resembled some true map only in outline.

• ■ •

After having roamed for about a week, going to a succession of cheap, dirty hotel rooms in the center of Athens, one afternoon when the poetical sunshine of the city was mixing with the smell of drug addicts' urine Karl found himself surrounded by three Albanians with angry faces. One of them ordered him not to move and, eyes glowing, pressed a knife against his throat. The other two, emptying his pockets with the dexterity of circus jugglers, took the few dollars he had on him as well as that masterpiece of counterfeiting, his passport. Apparently these three "hunters" had followed Karl as he rambled through the streets of Athens in the style of both beggar and daydreamer. They believed their compatriot's pockets were filled with dollar bills. Overcome with disappointment when they realized that their loot was so meager, the robbers wrinkled their lips. "He's worthless, this guy," one of them maintained as though estimating the value of some merchandise. They shoved him down violently against the pavement and distanced themselves rapidly, like circus acrobats departing the ring after completing their act.

Trembling with fear, Karl stood up. "Robbers!" he shouted in Albanian, after which he felt as though the consonants and vowels issuing from his mouth had been transformed into a boomerang landing as a slap on his own face. Without comprehending this, he himself had slapped his face as a means of recuperating.

• ■ •

The moment he crossed the border with his false visa, Karl thought that his life must resemble an extraordinary experiment. Despite not knowing what awaited him on the other side, the feeling of boundless freedom that he was tasting for the first time in his life intensified his imagination and intoxicated his senses. Far from his former relationships and his past, he would be able, he thought, to create himself anew from nothing, to leave forever behind him his country's dissolution, his past, his peculiar family, his authoritarian father, and that life of his in Ters — all so desperately predictable.

However, just a few days after he crossed the border, humiliated by a fellow countryman's threatening knife, his heart was overcome by fear and a mortifying sense of failure. He was not made to cross borders, he now thought. He was not made to create himself out of nothing. He was simply a loser and as such the only thing worth doing for him was to go back to his dismantled country, humiliated and defeated, to be restored to his past, his peculiar family, authoritarian father, and that life of his there in Ters — all so desperately predictable.

Karl decided to turn himself over voluntarily to the Greek police. On his own he would climb into one of those police paddy wagons, termed four-wheeled cells by the Albanian refugees who filled them daily. As these refugees traveled back toward the Albanian border, expelled by Greece as illegitimate, they would gaze with doleful eyes through windows covered with barbed wire, like wild beasts captured in a trap that they had set for themselves.

• ■ •

At dawn on November 4th, 1991, Karl was in Omonoia Square with furrowed brow, ruffled hair, wearing a black cotton jacket and gray cotton trousers, his eyes stinging from lack of sleep, his stomach aching from anguish and hunger. In the middle of this unattractive square filled with Albanian refugees, he resembled some Statue of the Defeated Loser.

He was ready to return to Ters.

Like a victim that offers itself of its own free will to the hunter, Karl was waiting for the shadow of some Greek policeman to approach him. He had sketched the entire scene in his mind. The policeman, extending his hand toward him in a disparaging manner, just as the garbage collector extends his hand toward trash, would yank him toward the black four-wheeled cell into which Karl would obediently climb with bowed head, disgusted by the policeman and all the more by himself.

The silhouette of a petite woman approached him. She was wearing a coffee-colored leather jacket over a light blue blouse; her hair was black, her eyes blue, her neck wrapped in a delicate silk kerchief. She said something to Karl in Greek but when she saw his dazed look she reached out with her hands and fingers. With her right hand she attempted to imitate a pruning hook and with the left hand a bush. Then the hand forming the pruning hook passed quickly over the hand forming the bush. To Karl it seemed as though one hand was imitating a knife, the other a human head.

At first he thought that this woman with the delicate silk kerchief had gone out of her mind. Or maybe he was the loony one and the sight of the woman moving her hands in that inexplicable manner was simply a figment of his imagination. However, a few seconds later when he observed the puzzlement in her eyes, her knitted brows, her large eyes attempting to convey to him a message he did not understand, he felt that he was dealing with a normal human being. "Italian, French, English, Spanish, Russian?" Karl murmured, attempting to find a common language. *"Français?"* the unknown woman asked. *"Oui, français,"* he replied. The exact moment that the unknown woman finally lowered her hands and said to Karl, *"Je cherche un jardinière pour mon jardin,"*[3] a black paddy wagon stopped a few yards from them. The Albanian refugees began running away like stray dogs sensing some approaching threat.

There was no time to lose. He had to choose between the paddy wagon and the unknown woman who spoke French.

Her name was Kleio.

When Karl left Ters, my heart filled with grievance, my eyes with tears. I knew he would not return in six months as he had promised. I felt the parting was

3. "I'm looking for a gardener for my garden."

for life. After he left, I conceived in my mind a theory that I still believe today. People in this world divide into two types: loyalists and absconders, those who endure and those who desert. To be loyal to your city, to your country, when everyone is abandoning it, to love it when everyone is denying it, that for me is the supreme human virtue.

Ever since our borders opened and people bolted away, I have heard about absconders and have read many accounts of them. Some come back and relate stories of humiliation in the places where they went. Others, regretting they returned, depart once again. Still others say that they are burning from nostalgia yet cannot return; their soul belongs here, they say, but their body belongs there. Indeed, many swear they will never return. They say Ters is a rotten town that gives you nothing but sorrow, poverty, gossip, and dust. So I wonder, since they abandoned Ters, what they could have found where they went.

I have seen various European cities. I greatly like their beauty, cleanliness, wealth. Yet it is only here in Ters that I sense my own self when I go to sleep and when I awake, when I am sad and when I rejoice, when I feel hopeful and when hopeless, when I have dreams and when I fear what comes next . . .

• 3 •

Even 15 years later, no matter where they were or what they were doing — walking in the streets of Athens, drinking wine, suffering from a summer heatwave, or awakening when they had run out of words and lacked anything more to say — Kleio and Karl would remember that strange encounter in Omonoia Square. Like two actors repeating their stage roles, these two imitated, revived, and reexperienced their gestures when, on that November morning, they had encountered each other for the first time. They repeated the words they had spoken, confessed the silent thoughts they had experienced. Both liked to imagine their meeting as something outlined in advance by the so mysteriously dramatic, so invisibly playful hand of fate.

Kleio would say that she had distinguished Karl among the crowd of hungry refugees as though pinpointing a treasure in the dark. It was something in the way he stood that differentiated him from the others, something in his glance ("Yes, yes, in your glance above all! Why are you laughing?"). What's more, she would say, it was because that morning Karl resembled a leaf at the mercy of a fierce wind owing to that special style of his, halfway between beggar and daydreamer, which had made the three robbers single him out. In Kleio's mind, this rare combination of need and innocence had displaced the instinctive fear that one person feels concerning another person. Also, a male whose style is halfway between beggar and daydreamer awakens in a female's soul something between the maternal instinct and uncontrollable curiosity.

• ■ •

It was a quirk of fate that brought Kleio to Omonoia Square that morning. Or, more exactly, it was her own quirk involving heads or tails. Her decision to look for a gardener among Albanian refugees in the center of Athens was more or less a way for her to get back at her deceased mother.

Her eighty-year-old mother had died of cancer in Athens's Evangelismos Hospital only a few weeks before Kleio accidentally came to know Karl. And a few days before her mother left mortal life, she had whispered in her daughter's ear: "Beware the Albanians because they kill you!" Kleio, stunned, gazed at this woman so debilitated by the incurable disease, viewed her closed eyes and her parched lips that seemed to have uttered those words as though raving in sleep. She had uttered that sentence, "Beware the Albanians because they kill you!" almost like a command, just as she had done throughout her life. For 43 consecutive years her oppressive presence had gouged out Kleio's life like a sculptor's chisel attacking marble. But among all the innumerable commands that the mother had attempted to impose upon her daughter throughout her life, it was specifically this one concerning the Albanians that Kleio wished passionately to contravene, like someone violating the inviolable.

As for Karl, what brought him close to Kleio by chance was an absurd combination of circumstances. Most of all it was his desire to cross borders, to go as far away as possible in a search for that invisible center of selfhood that had been violently displaced on the day of his mother's suicide. When he traversed the Greek border, Karl kept dreaming that he would journey far away, as far away as his feet and imagination could bring him. Yet his journey stopped on that November morning in Omonoia Square when he met this unknown woman almost as old as his mother.

What more than anything else directed each to the other's life, however, was perhaps the irresistibly strong appeal of loneliness. Kleio carried with her the loneliness of a woman with ruined dreams and hopes, of someone approaching the inevitable stage of life in which women's faith in their femininity begins irreparably to waver. Karl carried within himself the loneliness of a fugitive who yearns to leave the past behind so that he may create himself anew out of nothing. He had crossed the frontier and arrived in an unknown world coveted by him but not understood. In just a few days, that unknown world had frightened him, made him feel humiliated, defeated, abandoned, unwanted.

Karl had arrived as a ruin. Kleio awaited him as a refuge.

For hours on end I keep asking myself: Where in the world has Karl wandered to? Has he gained more than I have — I who have remained faithful to Ters? Has he perhaps grown wiser, richer, happier?

Now, after so many years, I see my brother and have the impression that he is a person completely free and absolutely lost . . . Karl rejected Ters for other cities, rejected his language for other languages, departed far from his family and homeland hoping to discover the solace of family and homeland elsewhere . . .

I often think that Karl suffers from the same self-destructive illness that has always affected Albanians. For centuries the Albanian was a wanderer, a runaway, a mercenary abroad. The Albanian easily forgets his homeland and devotes himself zealously to foreign homelands. The Albanian has aided Turkey, Greece, Italy, Egypt, but has rarely aided his own homeland. People now say that Enver H. made a mistake in closing our borders for half a century . . . Indeed, perhaps he did overdo it. Yet the intention was not wrong: it saved the nation from disappearing. He wanted to make the Albanians connect themselves to their own soil, teach them to love their homeland, discipline them to construct a strong identity . . . What the Albanians have always lacked is love for their nation. That, I fear, is also lacking in Karl . . .

4

Kleio's house and neglected garden (where Karl, not having the slightest idea about horticulture, bloodied his hands that November morning pruning bushes and the twigs of a wild rose) was a single-story detached structure surrounded by five- and six-story apartment buildings in an Athens neighborhood called Nea Smyrna. Until the beginning of the 1960s, all the homes in the neighborhood were the same as Kleio's: single-story residences with a small garden usually in back of the house.

After this came the age of the Concrete Epidemic, as Kleio's mother called it. All the single-story residences in the neighborhood disappeared within a few years. Purchased by contractors, they were replaced by multistory apartment buildings. Only the house occupied by Kleio's mother withstood the offers and pressures of the contractors, who wished to cover every inch of land with concrete.

Kleio's mother was a cantankerous woman who was generally annoyed regarding the present and nostalgic regarding the past. Her very special childhood years were spent in Smyrna, one of the Mediterranean's most cosmopolitan cities, which had been burned soon after World War I by Turkish irregulars when the Greek army retreated in defeat. Her family had been exterminated in the hellish flames that enwrapped the city. Only her mother and this daughter, a nine-year-old child, had managed to emerge alive. They reached Piraeus harbor having crossed the Aegean on a rotting fishing smack filled to suffocation by refugees who had lost everything. Left behind them besides their ancestors' graves were family members now burned to ashes by the flames, trampled to death by the fleeing mob, or simply missing. They hoped to return in a few days or even in weeks to bury their dead at least. They never did return. In front of them they found a new land they did not know and inhabitants who viewed them with suspicion and hostility.

Athens never managed to captivate Froso (that was Kleio's mother's name). It struck her as very provincial and its inhabitants as bitter and crude — people who did not even know how to cook, she would say. In her mind, Athens remained the opposite of Smyrna. The only time she felt sympathy for her new city was during its occupation by the merciless Germans and when the civil war broke out and Greeks began maniacally to kill Greeks after the occupiers left, filling the streets of Athens with bullets and blood.

Her mistrust of Athens, obtained all at once when she set foot there, had been intensified into abhorrence when the city began to be transformed into an urban monstrosity of concrete. The proclivity of the colonels' Junta for concrete and construction was the major reason why Froso hated those colonels. After the Junta's fall, she nevertheless continued to curse the concrete and the apartment buildings that were being built around her single-story private home. By curse after curse she reached as far as the poor Albanian refugees who suddenly flooded Greece at the beginning of the 1990s and worked endless hours for meager pay mixing cement to build these apartment houses, heaving one floor on top of another.

• ■ •

After her divorce, Kleio had returned to her mother's home, to the single-story private dwelling where she had grown up, to the building that had withstood the pressure of circumstances. She and her husband had spent 18 years together until one morning he told her that he was in love with another woman very much younger than either of them. They then separated without hysteria and screams — by "uncontested divorce" as it is termed in legal language. Kleio felt so devastated that she lacked the strength to come to grips with all the debilitating and humiliating legal proceedings needed to make her husband's life as difficult as possible — procedures that were nothing more than a legitimate, civilized version of archaic revenge and hate. She spent innumerable days and nights locked within herself, weeping bitterly and downing one glass of whiskey after another while listening to melancholy music, swallowing antidepressant pills, and cursing chiefly herself. On the day she received the divorce certificate in her hands she felt exactly like the pillaged, fire-consumed Smyrna.

• ■ •

"It's your fault your husband abandoned you," her mother told her with the customary expression on her face, that of the supreme critic. Throughout

Kleio's life, her mother had practiced this same "art": how to make her daughter feel guilty — guilty for marrying a man whom her mother had never approved of, guilty for not dressing as her mother wished, guilty for not knowing how to cook as was proper for a genuine Smyrniótissa, guilty because her legs were not as straight and lovely as Froso's had been in her youth, guilty for a thousand and one reasons, big and small, reasonable and unreasonable. Her mother was capable of making her feel guilty even because Kleio could not spawn children, and even for the fact that around her large, bright blue eyes had appeared the first wrinkles that reveal the menacing onslaught of time.

• ■ •

Kleio was aware that she had put her head in the noose regarding her husband because she had devoted herself to him without constraint. Leaving her own concerns in a shadow, she made his dreams paramount. She had followed him uncomplainingly to Paris, the city where he wished to complete his doctorate because his idol, the psychiatrist Jacques Lacan, had been born there and had also died there. Afterwards, when she had grown accustomed to Paris, loved it, and hoped they would stay, he told her that such a future was impossible, that they needed to return, that he was suffering from unbearable nostalgia, was incapable of living without Greece's unique light and the smell of its blue sea. Kleio prepared the valises of return, again uncomplainingly. They came back to an Athens where prosperity and the mania for consumption had suddenly invaded Greek life. Among other things, people had discovered the charm of psychoanalysis. One day, on his office's psychoanalytic couch, her former husband discovered a twenty-year-old, a patient of his with whom he fell in love, contrary to all the rules of psychoanalysis. "Love demolishes every norm of science!" he told Kleio with tearful eyes. The bastard!

• ■ •

During the four years they lived in Paris, thanks to the Paris-Brussels railway on which they traveled together almost every week, Kleio had acquired some stamina regarding trains. Without trains one cannot understand European history. That continent's good and bad, its bright and dark days, are connected in one way or another with train tracks and stations. She had begun then to devour historical books and novels in which protagonists and trains are related. Her sudden passion had surprised her husband, who had tried (without success) to find some relationship between Kleio's perseverance regarding trains and Lacan's feminine *jouissance*. In the end their marriage ran off its rails, having degenerated into a phantom railway. Kleio then returned to her mother's single-story home and her beloved bedroom with the small garden visible out back.

She named it "The Train Room."

Karl entered Kleio's life a few years after she had separated from her husband, a few weeks after her mother's death. Handsome, young, strong and at the same time easily conquered, thirsty to run toward the future, to discover a new homeland, a new self and identity, he entered her life as an unpredictable alteration blossoming like a wild orchid.

Two weeks after their meeting in Omonoia Square, Karl and Kleio were touching and licking each other with pleasure in The Train Room, its walls covered with old posters showing tracks, passengers, inspectors, boisterous railway stations in Italy, rusted train cars abandoned in Siberia. Karl's first book, entitled Short Train-Diary, had its beginning in those afternoons filled with their orgasms and dreams — he aged 22, she 43 . . .

Karl liked to repeat certain ideas that I continue to find difficult to understand. For example, I remember him once saying to me, "I cannot feel love for any nationality. The only thing I am capable of loving is humanity, quite apart from the nationality to which humans belong." In Albania and elsewhere today, people are ashamed to say that they love their nationality and identity. Hatred for nationality and identity has become fashionable. The greater your hatred, the more liberated, cosmopolitan, and avant-garde you are considered. I am neither liberated, cosmopolitan, nor avant-garde. I do not desire my nation to become a historical relic. If the nation dies, what will replace it — an empire without an identity, without a race, without boundaries between languages and ethnicities, male and female, a chaos where everyone will mix with everyone else, where your left hand will ignore what your right hand is doing? . . .

• 5 •

That magical world map — the one Karl held in his mind when he set out beyond borders for an unknown land — had acquired the shape of a woman's body: Kleio's. She had become his compass and mirror, pleasure and refuge, shield and guide. If she had not entered his life almost contrary to any logic, Karl's journey would not have terminated in Greece. Perhaps he would have continued blindly toward the West, to France or Italy, or most likely he would have returned to Ters. Now, thanks to this encounter, he was an illegal refugee in Greece in love with a Greek woman.

But even refugees in love require a residence permit.

The words "residence permit" entered Karl's life together with the autumn rains and Athens's noisy streets. In the passage of time those two words would be transformed into phantoms haunting him in even the darkest corners of his sleep. It was paradoxically during his most favorable moments that they made him feel susceptible, temporary, and foreign.

The first residence permit he obtained was thanks to a cousin of Kleio's who worked in the central offices of the Athenian Police Department. It was thin, microscopical, a tiny booklet colored blue like the national flag nailed to the Greek customs house when Karl was waiting in No Man's Land. "It is fortunate you have a Greek name," Kleio's policeman cousin told him. Almost the same had been said to him by Goni son of

Fatime, the counterfeiter. If his name had not been "Greek," to receive a residence permit he would have needed to change it to a new, more "appropriate" name that would not have provoked the authorities' enmity and the local residents' suspicion. Thousands of Albanians were changing their names just as people change soiled clothes after work, hoping in this way to acquire that magical something, a residence permit, or at least to be saved a deportation journey in the black four-wheeled cell, like captured wild animals enclosed in a pit. By zealously changing their names, Albanian refugees were refuting the theory that those who are weak fall prey to being furiously captured owing to their name and identity. In reality, it is the strong of this world who view their identity as higher and waterproof, something that resembles a daring vessel that continually sets sail for exotic, wild places in a glorious civilizing mission against barbarians. The weak generally see their identity as modeling clay or as a rowboat leaking water in open seas.

"This residence permit needs to be renewed every year," Kleio's policeman cousin added, stressing the words "every year" as a means of conveying the exceptional value contained. As he stuffed into his pocket the envelope containing his formidable gratuity, he resembled the customs policeman at the border, with eyes of an overfed cat. The moment Karl took the magical something into his grip, he stared at the policeman's hands in the same way he had also stared at the hands of Goni son of Fatime — with gratitude and contempt.

PART 3

• 1 •

A writer's mind often resembles a cemetery. Most of the stories and characters fashioned by such a mind usually return like midnight shadows to the mysterious darkness of their source. Those that survive are very few. If they do survive, remaining fortunate, they will be transformed into words, sentences, paragraphs. This is what happened when Karl's mind conceived Syndrom von Frontier, the fictitious tragicomic character of his second book, which his intellect began to design one afternoon in November when he and Kleio reached Sebnitz, a small, quiet town in Saxony near the German-Czech border. As part of East Germany after World War II, the town became a frontier guard post comprising a portion of the Cold War's impenetrable border (although one now passes it in a carefree manner with passport or official stamp). Traveling toward Sebnitz via Thuringia, Kleio and Karl had encountered a poster with the sign "Halt! Hier Grezne" and other remnants of the militarized "dead zone" between East and West Germany on the border that for almost half a century had divided Europe in half. However, despite these few old traces of a recent past, no one in that region possessed an appetite to talk any longer about the Cold War border and olden times. The truth is that everyone in Europe was in a hurry to forget the Cold War, in the West because that period induced nostalgia ("life then was more foreseeable," most people whispered) whereas in the East because people could not bear to encounter themselves in history's mirror.

Sebnitz, located in the middle of a green valley surrounded by picturesque knolls, is a beautiful, wealthy, totally clean old town famous for its artificial flowers. In the winter, when the snow keeps tourists far away from the town's exotic forests, the place with its two- and three-story buildings, like doll houses, resembles a silent cathedral. The clamorous mob visits the small town only on weekends during that season, when Germans come from the surrounding cities and regions, drink beer until they have forgotten how many bottles they consumed, eat sausages with pretzel dumplings, clink their glasses like boxers joining their fists in the ring, and enjoy themselves singing old songs. Near midnight, when they have reached full exuberance, they take their expensive automobiles and, crossing the Czech border, head for Libido Borderless, the most celebrated brothel of the frontier zones, filled with low-priced girls from eastern Europe.

• ■ •

Kleio had chosen Sebnitz so she could photograph the town's old train station and celebrate with Karl the anniversary of their chance meeting in Omonoia Square. "The years pass quickly," Kleio ventured as she took a shot of the railway tracks. It was early afternoon and drizzling. The Sebnitz station was almost empty, with only three or four elderly men waiting then on the platform and looking impatiently at their watches even though trains in that corner of Europe usually arrive on schedule. "They seem like matches expecting to be struck for the last time in their lives, don't they?" Karl asked Kleio, nodding toward them.

As they were drinking beer in one of the pubs in the small town's central square that evening, Kleio spoke again about the quickly passing years. When they had met, time had come to a standstill between them like a magically suspended bridge. On that bridge, they embraced, undressed each other, licked each other's face and sexual organs, each thirstily swallowing the other just as the Germans were swallowing their beer in that pub. Now, however, after 15 years together, Kleio viewed time as lying in wait like a minefield. She felt she was walking along this field fearful it would explode into the air together with herself and the hope that Karl would always be hers. Leaning her head against Karl's shoulder, she gently bit his ear, as she did whenever she desired to have sex with him. "I want you to fuck me the whole night long," she whispered in a voice intoxicated with hedonism and alcohol.

• ■ •

The following morning while they were drinking warm tea in their hotel room, Kleio declared, "Karl, my body no longer attracts you." She pronounced those words with the certainty with which a person tells time. Afterwards, to hide her agitation, she turned her back and rushed into the bathroom.

"I'm going to take a shower," she said in a trembling voice.

Naked under the warm water, she thought once again about their difference in age, her menopause that had begun a short time before, the panic she felt upon seeing the first gray hairs between her legs, the wrinkles that had thickened and widened around her eyes, her skin that was losing its former vivacity. Recently she often returned to the memory of their first sex in the Train Room: Karl's tight skin, his strong hands, his heart beating as though attempting to emerge from inside, his tongue that licked her beautiful breasts and hips, his sigh of pleasure when he had ejaculated his hot semen onto her belly.

From that night onward, Kleio had become his muse and refuge. In an environment hostile to foreigners, especially to Albanians, she had taught him the secrets of sex and of the Greek language. She had become the faithful reader and corrector of his manuscripts, had worshipped him and had given him self-confidence. She had dedicated herself to him, had granted him all that she possessed — home, friends, money, envelopes containing gratuities for renewals of his residence permit — so that he might succeed. She had kept a distance even from close friends when they noted sarcastically that Kleio "fell in love with an Albanian." She had not hesitated to sacrifice all of this in order not to lose Karl.

One summer evening, however, while they were sitting in their garden and talking about their first meeting, Karl mentioned the word "gratitude." It was as though her whole being then crumpled. The word "gratitude" uttered from Karl's lips meant that in his mind their relationship had already entered the past, was something belonging to history, a precious relic in the museum of dead liaisons.

Kleio did not desire Karl to view her with gratitude for being his savior. What she wanted was Karl to continue to see her with the same fiery longing and need with which his eyes had viewed her when they first met, with that sensuous gaze that encompassed her like a wild garden when they experienced sex together for the first time in the Train Room. She wanted the two of them to keep sleeping naked together every night, Karl to continue dreaming he would one day become a famous author, she to remain his muse. Together they would earn money for trips to the small towns and villages of Europe involving train stations forgotten by time and humanity.

• ■ •

Just as birds sense an imminent earthquake, Kleio realized when she had first sensed that Karl was deceiving her — four years, six months, and thirteen days after their initial meeting. Waves of jealousy flooded her heart like the billows of a rough sea sinking a dilapidated rowboat. At first she decided to separate from him, to expel him from the detached house with its small garden which Karl had eventually learned to tend. Later, a voice inside her, perhaps an illusory power, had convinced her that Karl's infidelity was the tax she was required to pay for the abyss separating her age from his. Subsequently she created a type of emotional shield, a conscious insensitivity and naiveté opposing the signs of Karl's infidelity: those novel perfumes, inane justifications when he failed to return to the house at night, forgotten slips of paper in his pockets with telephone numbers and women's names.

• ■ •

Beneath the shower's warm water, Karl's naked body touched Kleio's. She felt Karl's fingers between her legs and her body quivered as though pierced by an electric current. "I want you inside," she whispered to him . . . A half hour later they were stretched out side by side on the bed, silent, wrapped in still wet white towels. They could hear from outside the clamor of a demonstration's shouting. Puzzled, Karl jumped off the bed and went to the room's window. A throng of angry people in the street was passing by at that moment shouting rhythmically and holding in their hands photos of women in burkas, German flags, and the slogan *Schließt die Grenzen!* (Close the Borders!). "I think it's a demonstration against refugees," said Karl, troubled. Kleio said nothing; she had turned face-down on the bed, burying her features in the pillow. "Karl, I know you cheat on me with other women," she uttered shortly in a fading voice. "But do not abandon me." She had found the unthinkable courage to pronounce those words after so many years, her voice betraying a woman who had displayed the most mortifying compromises in an effort to retain Karl's close presence, which filled her days and nights with meaning.

• ■ •

Two months following their night at Sebnitz, Kleio awoke on their bed in the Train Room and Karl was gone. She jumped out of bed so quickly that she almost lost her balance. She hoped for a moment that she would hear some sound in the house, something that would convey his presence. Occasionally Karl would get up during the night and rummage through the kitchen for his favorite chocolates. The house was absolutely silent. "Karl, where are you?" Kleio called in a trembling voice. No answer. She put on her silk bathrobe, walked quickly down the passageway to the toilet and knocked on its closed door. "Karl, are you inside?" He was not there. She crossed the sitting room, opened the house's back door and went out into the garden, her hair in disarray. She saw the small bench they had placed in the garden's center a few years earlier. She remembered the night when, half intoxicated, they had made love on this bench, entirely indifferent to whether they might be seen from the windows of the adjoining apartment building. The bench was empty. Outdoors was cold. Reentering the house, she rushed with frantic steps into the kitchen, straightening her robe with trembling hands. On the table where they usually ate breakfast, she found a note. Karl had abandoned her at night, just as the prodigal son abandons his paternal home.

• ■ •

Kleio tried to find Karl by telephone, to make him change his mind and return to the Train Room.

"How could you flee at night like a burglar?" she asked him.

"I'll come to get my things," he abruptly replied.

His tone of voice at the other end of the line was distant and formal.

Karl returned for the last time to the one-story house and gathered up his belongings.

The two of them sat for a moment in the sitting room opposite each other as they had sat countless times all those years, this time embarrassed, like strangers, without looking at each other's eyes.

"Why did you leave at night, Karl? Do you want to live with another woman?" she asked him.

Karl said nothing. He looked at his wristwatch to escape her steady glance.

"Karl, tell me what you want and I'll give it to you," she said after a short silence.

"I myself don't know what I want," he answered, trying again with his eyes to escape Kleio's.

"I know," Kleio declared.

Karl laughed sarcastically as though wishing to ask her how she, better than he himself knew, could know what he desired.

"You are suffering from departure sickness," Kleio told him.

"Departure sickness?" he repeated like someone caught unprepared.

"You are searching for absolute freedom. But that exists only for God (if God exists), not for mortals like you and me," said Kleio.

Kleio had wrapped around her neck the same kerchief she was wearing when they first met. Her sleepless swollen eyes and her slightly trembling hands made her seem suddenly very old at that moment.

"And you, what do you suffer from?" Karl asked her somewhat belligerently.

"At this moment I am suffering from an inability to understand why you abandoned our bed in the middle of the night," said Kleio, her voice trembling. "Karl," she added irritatingly, "a wild, mean crowd is waiting for you out there. Without me, you'll be lost."

"I need to go," Karl responded.

"Don't you want to see the garden for the last time?" she asked him again in a pleading voice.

Karl shook his head, indicating refusal.

"Those who suffer from departure sickness usually dare not look back," Kleio said, her voice again conveying irritation.

"We have spoken enough," said Karl, his voice cold and formal. His facial expression had hardened into the features of someone trying persistently to deny reality.

For the first time, his presence made Kleio feel afraid.

• ■ •

Kleio continued to hope that Karl would return. At first she sent him a letter in which she reminded him of their first meeting in Omonoia Square, of their travels, their insomniac nights during which she corrected his manuscripts, their lovemaking at dawn (ah, how lascivious, what exquisite sexual pleasure following wakeful nights!). Later on she sent him a second letter, an angry one regarding the fact that he had vanished from the house during the night in that unreasonable manner so humiliating for her. Then a third letter, very long, in which she attempted to analyze their relationship from its start, the chance misunderstandings, the repressions, the acrimonious fears that each of them had amassed silently over the years, unconsciously, without managing ever to talk openly about them. "For example, the fact that I never learned Albanian was a big mistake on my part. A failure like that could have injured you," she wrote him, "making you think, even if subconsciously, that our relationship was not an equivalent one." Kleio proposed that they go together to a psychologist treating couples or separately to a psychoanalyst. Karl did not answer. Nor did he return to the one-family home and garden. Kleio therefore felt as she had years earlier owing to her divorce: like a pillaged, fire-consumed Smyrna.

The last words in their history were written by Kleio one night when Karl's loss had finally become permanent in her mind and the pain from his absence had finally grown unbearable: "I loved you in every language. I hate you in every language." It was owing to Karl that she had uttered the word "hate" for the very first time. As for him, he knew that without Kleio's protective, adoring glance he would never have reached as far as he had done; nor would he ever have felt sufficient self-confidence to abandon the Train Room at night. Thinking that Kleio hated him troubled him in the way a person is troubled when he views his shattered image in the fragments of a broken mirror.

• ■ •

It was with Anna, a girl ten years younger than him, that Karl continued his life. They had met when she asked him for an interview concerning her diploma thesis (its title: "The Sexual Ambiguity of Bilingualism among Immigrants"). A few days after meeting for the interview, a few months before Karl traveled to Sebnitz with Kleio, Anna and Karl ended up in bed. Anna's eyes, like Kleio's, were large; her fingers, like Kleio's, were long; her hair, unlike Kleio's, was short.

They rented an apartment in Exarcheia on the fourth floor of an apartment building, one of those structures that Kleio's mother reviled. With its brand-new elevator and an elderly man with his pair of hysterical dogs as neighbors, that minuscule dwelling housed three months of impassioned sex and six months of wild arguments often accompanied by broken dishes.

Their disputes commenced one quiet evening as both, seated on their apartment's couch, were watching a television documentary about the attack several years earlier on the Twin Towers in New York City. When the screen showed the two lofty towers converted into ghastly torches, Anna declared that the Americans had learned a good lesson that day. At first she did not comprehend how Karl had frozen when he heard her words. Facing his surprised look, she tried to explain to him that although she felt great sorrow for the people who had died, the collapse of the Twin Towers, that symbol of savage capitalism, could be considered positive. "First and foremost it was something truly affirmative: an attack against globalization." Continuing with the serious appearance of someone undertaking a meaningful geopolitical analysis, she added, "Second, the spoiled Americans whose only God is money finally felt under the skin the meaning of pain and death."

"Thousands of civilians were murdered," mumbled Karl.

"Do you know how many hundred thousands of civilians the Americans have murdered and are still murdering?" Anna asked as though she had long awaited Karl's reaction.

This struck him momentarily as though he were hearing his father's voice issuing from the mouth of a beautiful woman. His father had often asked, "Do you know how many hundred thousands of innocent people the Americans have murdered and are still murdering?" Verbatim!

Like a disease attacking someone who considers himself immune, Anna's variation caught Karl unprepared. At first he thought that his mind was playing some ugly game in comparing Anna to his father and he told himself that he must promptly dismiss that comparison. He must smile, embrace Anna, kiss her lovely mouth, glue his body on top of hers. Sex, he told himself, must surpass every ideological stupidity and misunderstanding. However, instead of sucking in her lips, his mouth emitted words that surprised even him:

"Are you really so misanthropic?"

Anna looked at him with a startled expression, almost goggle-eyed, trying to pinpoint some trace of humor in Karl's words. His glance, however, was exceedingly grim.

"Are you out of your mind?" she asked him, placing her finger on her temple.

"How can someone be so full of hate?" Karl said, raising his voice.

"You jerk-off!" Anna then screamed, her face bright red with anger. Jumping up from the couch, she grabbed one of the porcelain dishes on the table and threw it with all her might onto the floor. A multitude of broken plates regularly accompanied their innumerable arguments.

Occasionally after their earsplitting quarrels they found slips of paper with the strange signature

"ZZ" under their apartment's door, written by the neighbor with the two hysterical dogs. The language employed by the neighbor was even stranger: "I kindly request that you solve your differences in a manner the effect of which is not so negative upon my two dogs. P.S. My dogs are the border collie species of Welsh pedigree, and they relapse into a wild rage every time you argue. ZZ."

Karl and Anna coexisted for another six months in a condition of erotic bipolar disorder, the extremes of their relationship advancing with insane rapidity from one antipode to the other, from savage quarreling to ardent vows of eternal love. At first they endeavored via forgetfulness to bury their collision regarding the Twin Towers. It is absurd, they said, for one of us to butcher the other owing to something that bears no relation whatsoever to our everyday lives. Nevertheless, despite the thousands of miles separating them from the Twin Towers, despite the entire ocean between them and the victims who had died there, it was apparent that their relationship had been sacrificed in an unreasonable manner by the frightful event in New York City.

Unavoidably, their quarrels acquired a political tinge for reasons continually more insignificant. Anna's ideological narrations, according to which communism had never been correctly applied anywhere and ruthless capitalistic society should be overthrown by a new communist revolution, were considered by Karl as hypocritical nonsense made by people who daydreamed the overturn of the very system to which they owed their own well-being. Anna then called Karl "a slave of capitalism" and a "petit bourgeois." And when one day Karl said that Mao and Lenin were among the greatest criminals ever known in human history, Anna termed him "fascist" and "macho." That was the final act in their brief dramatic relationship. Taking her clothes and books, Anna left. Karl remained. Alone now in that minuscule apartment and without the broken plates and the slips of paper beneath the door, he continued to fashion the nature of Syndrom von Frontier, the creation of his imagination to which he would owe his subsequent fame as a "talented author" in Greece and elsewhere.

Every summer before serious illness prostrated our mother, we used to pass two months vacationing on the shores of the Adriatic. Mother adored the soft, sugar-white sand of Divjakë. If heaven exists, she used to say, Divjakë's sand must be there. "Heaven and hell are here on earth, Vali," Father would answer, and Mother would laugh. We truly lived in a heaven then. Open-air seaside movies, excursions to Pogradeci or to Mount Dajti, dinner at Pista, the restaurant next to La Seine, where Mom and Dad waltzed with other couples. As a child I felt indescribable pride seeing the degree of respect and admiration that people from Ters gave to my parents. Afterwards, Mother became seriously ill and everything grew difficult. Then came the arguments between Karl and Father. If I believed in the evil eye, I would say that somebody had cast a spell over our family.

I tried then to find some warmth in Karl, but he became increasingly more inaccessible and morose.

He spoke constantly about exiled individuals like Tower of Babel, and about political prisoners. "Do you realize that we live in a country that has become a jail," he persistently asked me, pointing toward the Mahalla[4] *of the Damned at the outskirts of Ters, the residence of those who had been banished. He wanted me to think in absolutely the same way. Naturally, I too was not pleased about the existence of exiles like Tower of Babel or of political prisoners like Crazy Pandi. But I kept wondering at the same time why they ended up in prison and we did not. Were they better than us, more honest? Of course not. After all, why should I feel guilty on their behalf, as Karl does? How could I feel closer to people like Tower of Babel, with whom I have no connection at all, than to my father? Why should I destroy my life because the lives of various people unknown to me have been destroyed? After all, life — apart from political regimes — is war, not an amusement park. Those who manage to survive and live are the strongest; others get involved in the trenches, fall in, and break their necks. Those who survive and stand up straight are smarter than those who fall in — that's now what I think. We are not exiled, nor has anyone threatened to toss us in jail. I don't understand why I ought to deny everything that is good and beautiful around us, as Karl has done. All things considered, I do not believe that I came into this world in order to change it.*

Since then I have understood that life for Karl has only two colors: black and white. He discovers life's

4. Mahalla: An Arabic word used throughout the Balkans to mean "neighborhood."

meaning by seeing only the black everywhere. He searches to find defects even in what is most perfect. Since then I have also understood that Karl suffers from megalomania; he thinks he has a mission to change the world. In that he is more similar to our father than I am, because our father also believed that he was going to change the world. In the end it was the world that changed him. Sooner or later the same will also happen to Karl . . .

• 2 •

Twenty-two years after crossing the Greek border with the fake visa made by Goni son of Fatime (whose soul was wandering now in the House of the Dead), Karl was considered a "successfully integrated immigrant" in the specialized terminology pertaining to "the integration of aliens." Having published three successful volumes, the third entitled *They Call Me Europe*, he was a writer whose personality and books were treated in numerous articles and positive reviews appearing in Greek and foreign newspapers. Sociologists who made their living by writing studies about immigrants in Greece used Karl as an excellent example to demonstrate that this country (from which people generally emigrated with gusto to every other point on the horizon) was not so bad for the foreigners who in the last 20 years had been coming to it from far and wide.

Readers often filled the auditoriums where his books were being presented. Sometimes they sighed with genuine admiration, "Oh, you don't seem at all like an Albanian." Although Karl continued to work as a receptionist at a central Athenian hotel (his chief talent being his linguistic skills) he belonged without question to one of the rarest categories of foreigners in Greece: those who had succeeded despite the certainty of failure in the imagination of native citizens.

Most of all, his readers displayed surprise at Karl's knowledge of Greek. Some told him that he spoke and wrote Greek better than they did; others asked him with curiosity and anxiety, "In which language do you dream?" Karl responded that the language in which he dreamed was a potpourri, a linguistic collage composed of the sounds of the six languages he spoke. The natives appeared confused by this answer. The most romantic would rather have Karl dream exclusively in Albanian (thereby confirming the theory that humans are born and die with only a single language and identity); others desired that he dream exclusively in Greek (thereby confirming the theory that barbarians are assimilated by a superior language and civilization). In each case, every time Karl said that he dreamed in a potpourri of languages, the majority of natives gave him a look that was difficult for anyone to decipher, one given by a questioner to an interlocutor who resembled a hybrid of genius and psychopath. The look given him by natives at those times reminded Karl of the way the citizens of Ters view the distinguished translator Tower of Babel, possessor of 20 living and dead languages, who as an exile within Ters swept the city's incessantly muddy streets. Inhabitants occasionally approached him and asked to be told in which language, of the many he knew, he dreamed. Tower of Babel would raise his eyes then to the sky over Ters and respond, "O people! my dreams are like a silent film."

• ■ •

The best indication that Karl truly belonged to the category of the "successfully integrated immigrant" was the multitude of letters filled with admiration he received from young Greek women (this never happens in the case of non-integrated immigrants). Some wrote that owing to his books their manner of viewing the immigrants around them had forever changed; others requested an autograph and still others flirted with him openly.

After the publication of his second book, the one with the fictitious character Syndrom von Frontier, Karl's life began to be filled with book presentations, interviews, and ephemeral sexual adventures while his heart was dominated for the first time by a liberating, confirmative sense of belonging.

Naturally, however, there were things reminding him that he was still a foreigner in this country: hostile glances of the civil servants every time he renewed his residence permit; words on television by Orthodox priests (chiefly the metropolitan bishops with their black robes and white beards) when they raged against foreigners, especially Albanians; racist slogans of the type "Albanian, you'll never become Greek!" shouted by hooligans at football matches or frequently written by anonymous trolls on his Facebook page. At such moments he regretted that he had failed to keep the promise he had given himself when he crossed the border. He thought that if he had not met Kleio, he would then have traveled probably as far as his legs could have carried him.

The speed and ease with which he banished his sadness regarding his failure to continue his journey beyond Greece meant that he felt increasingly less foreign. In this country where he had been living contrary to his imagination's plans, Karl now encountered more glances of admiration than of scorn, more of curiosity than distrust, more people who loved his books than who hated their author, more affection than rejection. He felt that he had at last discovered a new homeland where he could dream of the future, create a new identity, fall in love, live, experiment . . . and make mistakes.

Until the day when magic suddenly became nightmare — as in Russian folktales with the sorceress Baba Yaga — the day when he once again encountered the implacable glance of a fanatic resembling an incurable disease.

Karl believed he could become someone else, could exchange his identity with another person's. He believed he could become a Greek. Now he probably will think he has become an American. Or perhaps he thinks he has two or three identities, just as folks have two or three automobiles. But an identity is not an automobile. An identity is like a tree. If you uproot it from the soil it will dry out and rot. Frequently my father used to repeat the words of Count de Gobineau, "You're a foreigner in all countries of the world, except in France." Gobineau certainly said this about a Frenchman, but someone could say the same about Albanians: "You're a foreigner wherever you are, except in Albania." The Greek does not become Albanian; the Albanian does not become Greek. The American cannot become Chinese or the Chinese become American. On the surface you might probably become and appear whatever you wish, but only on the surface. In depth, where the primitive voice of nature gushes forth, you remain forever who you were at birth. One is born Albanian, Greek, American, or Chinese; one does not become them.

• 3 •

Everything began with an anonymous story that Karl published on his Facebook page. It was the story of an elderly Greek woman who had survived a massacre toward the end of World War II, the time when Europe was drowning in death, hunger, and hate. The irregulars of a Greek general named Zervas, fighting in the mountains of Epirus, decided to "clean up" the Albanian-speaking Muslim Tsamides who lived in the surrounding area — those whom the general accused of collaborating with the Germans as well as, mostly, those who were innocent. The general's troops were famous in that area not so much for resistance to the Germans as for the refrain they sang with full throats: *"No non-Christian will remain in this town / Every resister we shall mow him down."*

One day when hawser-thick rain was falling, the general collected his bravest of the brave and said to them, "The Germans exterminated the Jews; we shall exterminate the Albanians." Thus they set out, some dead drunk, others sober, some with legs trembling with eagerness, others with heels in pain from tramping, some with heavy hearts and others with bloodthirsty livers. They marched for hours until they reached their chosen destination, the beautiful seaside town called Parga. After slaughtering humans in the central square and animals in their stables, they beseeched the Virgin Mary to forgive their sins, to protect them from the evil eye, to care for their infant children in their cradles, to give to their sons strong balls, to their daughters rich bridegrooms, and to themselves extensive farmland and powerful voices enabling them to sing until breathless, *"No non-Christian will remain in this town / Every resister we shall mow him down."*

News about the Parga massacre spread faster than news about cholera. The Muslim Tsamides, from infants in the cradle up to oldsters grown tired of life, made a run for it, more frightened than the herd of cattle left behind, more darkened than even the black ashes heaped up in the hearths of the dwelling places they were abandoning.

It was the winter of 1945.

• ▪ •

The father of the elderly woman, a man as tall and thin as a stalk of bamboo, said, "We do not run away. Our dead are here, not across the border." They stayed put, even when the entire village begged them with tearful eyes to leave before death arrived, its brows as pitch-black as coal. They stayed put, she aged four at that time, together with three sisters. Afterwards everything happened quickly. The general's soldiers, with rifles and torches, reached their house around noontime. To begin, they set fire to the stable in the yard, which became wrapped in flames. The cow inside also caught fire. Bellowing from fear and pain, her body ablaze, she twirled in frenzy like a ballerina choreographed by Nijinsky. The cow gave up the ghost while dancing her frantic death-dance and the soldiers, seeing this, laughed until tears soaked the corneas of their goggling eyes.

"Now it's people's turn," whooped the truly bravest of the brave who led them, a man neither tall nor short, with a big head and two fingers missing from each of his small hands. Curses, shrieks, wild cheers in Greek and Albanian about death, sounds of the two languages a hopeless tangle swamping the house, yard, air, and fluttering above the wide wooden fence, expiring somewhere within the surrounding hills. Both slaughterers and slaughtered spoke and understood each language, Greek and Albanian, as often happens in the Balkans, where people with different religions who speak the same language, drink the same raki, sing the same songs, and fear the same evil eye suddenly begin to slaughter each other — the Balkans, where funereal dirges surpass every other form of art in their heartbreaking beauty.

• ■ •

They all died, bodies on one side, heads on the other — all except the four-year-old who, still alive, crawled on her belly amid the insane noise of the soldiers' bullets and glittering knife blades. She crawled beneath the home's large ottoman in a dark corner resembling the world's darkest night, roosting there like a half-dead bird where light did not find her.

She remained in that place without breathing a word until it seemed to her that she had been found in the darkness by her mother's bloody head, which crossed that scene of massacre and whispered to her, "You must live, my dearest!" The general's soldiers were looking around inside the house, breaking things, looting, overturning whatever they encountered in their way, and when they believed they had done their job blamelessly, they departed, brandishing their rifles in the air as well as their flasks of raki like the booty of triumph. Returning again to the place whence they had come, praying the Virgin to forgive them their sins, they continued loudly singing, *"No non-Christian will remain in this town / Every resister we shall mow him down."*

Motionless beneath the ottoman, the baby endured like a breathing corpse. She would have remained that way for several hours until she gave up the ghost had she not heard some steps at the doorway. These were not steps bringing death. A four-year-old child who has faced death understands how to distinguish human steps that bring life from those that do not. She began to cry, gasping. Echoing like a funereal church bell, her voice suffused the slaughterhouse.

The hands of a woman took her from the darkness where she lay. Lifting her into the air, the unknown woman whispered grimly into the child's ear, "Do not be afraid," while she wrapped her in a woolen blanket. Then, with movements just as grim as her voice and a stern glance resembling the heavy twilight then enwrapping the slaughterhouse, she gave the child to a man approximately 40 years old.

Starting with that night and every night thereafter, the child slept in the house of this unknown couple who lived in the adjoining village, occupied by Christian Arvanites, who drank the same raki as her father drank, who grieved just as her mother and sisters grieved — just like those who remained in the slaughterhouse unmourned and unburied because no one remained to mourn and bury them. On this same night that she escaped the jaws of death, she changed her name and religion, becoming Evangelia instead of Fatime, Christian instead of Muslim, and erased everything from her memory: her three sisters, her mother, her father, the unfortunate cow burning as though in a fireworks display. From that night onward her parents became those who had saved her life. Since this couple were unable to have children, neither sisters nor brothers existed in this new home of hers. She never revisited the slaughterhouse, not even in her dreams and nightmares, nor when she gave thanks to the Virgin for that miracle: life after death.

• ▪ •

The infant grew older, went to Athens, far from the slaughterhouse, married, gave birth to her own children. After many years, unexpectedly, memory rose up against the forgetfulness she had placed over herself like a tombstone. At first she believed the cause was the Albanian language brought to the house by an Albanian cleaning lady (who, each day after work, would telephone her son in Albania for a long time). These sounds of the language that she had voluntarily erased from memory got on her nerves, annoying her. With heavy heart she decided to fire the Albanian cleaning lady and replace her this time with a Filipina. Yet the imaginary figment of the slaughterhouse insisted on returning to her mind. The faces of her mother and sisters, also the knife blades glittering like devil's eyes, began to visit her not just in sleep but also when, awake, she was engaged in entirely habitual activities, drinking her morning coffee or estimating how much she would spend at the farmers' market . . .

• ■ •

She was certain it was the slaughterhouse specter that had delivered this cancer to her, igniting in her brain a conflagration just like the fire in the cow's stable. When one afternoon her oncologist, after exhaustive examinations that had lasted for weeks, told her, "I am sorry, but I must inform you that you have only a few more months to live," she decided not to fight any longer against the aroused memories.

In the beginning she narrated her story to a priest she had known for years at the Panaghia Chrysopolitissa church where she was accustomed to pray. When she finished her confession, he looked at her with a terrified gaze and said, "It is best, and God's will, that you take that story with you." However, to take her story with her wherever she would be going did not suit her. What if there she met her father, as tall and thin as a stalk of bamboo, her mother with doleful eyes, her three sisters with cut throats? She wished to leave her history behind her here, for those still alive. Instead of following the priest's advice, she discovered Karl and narrated to him what had happened.

• ■ •

Evangelia (formerly Fatime) discovered Karl thanks to Christos P., Karl's neighbor with the two hysterical dogs. Shortly after Karl and Anna separated, curiosity urged Karl to knock on the door of the strange neighbor who slid a signed "ZZ" slip of paper under his neighbors' door every time Karl and Anna argued with broken dishes. When they first met, Christos informed Karl that he was "a solitary rowboat that continually leaks water in the middle of the sea but does not sink." In his long eventful life he had managed to include 25 years in Istanbul (he was born there into a Greek family), 15 years in Paris, where he had married twice, and seven years in West Berlin before the wall came down, where he had married a third time. Eighty years of life, three marriages, three divorces, two daughters, neither of whom lived near him in Greece. In this first meeting of theirs Karl also discovered that ZZ were the initial letters of the names of Christos's two dogs, the two large border collies that ran around aggressively in their master's ample, messy apartment. Their names were Zabladowski (a character in Dr. Seuss's film The 5,000 Fingers of Dr. T.) and Zorro (from The Mark of Zorro starring Tyrone Power as Zorro the fox).

Karl and Christos came close like two pedigree dogs that, smelling each other, feel a mutual attraction. Their significant difference in age made their friendship even more peculiar. Christos viewed in Karl the son that he never spawned (he had two daughters, one living with her husband in Denmark, the other, a lesbian, living with her partner in Paris). In Karl's eyes, Christos was an urban version of the character Zorba. An otorhinolaryngologist, passionate about history, he had worked since young childhood and had lived zealously, traveled zealously, read books zealously, made many mistakes zealously, had loved and hated zealously. At the head of the list of ideas despised by Christos P. was that of the nation-state, which he scorned in a manner almost anthropomorphic, like a prisoner scorning his torturer. "The nation-state, that straitjacket given us by history to wear," he used to declaim, huffing and puffing, causing one to assume he was speaking about something that happened to his own family. Afterwards, as though journeying in a time machine replete with nostalgia, he would tally one by one the Mediterranean cities in which at some point the religions, languages, and different ethnicities lived side by side in a single form of bustling, chaotic cosmopolitanism, under the shelter of some boundless empire. "Alexandria, once upon a time cosmopolitan, today a ghost town; Smyrna, once upon a time cosmopolitan, today a ghost town; Thessaloniki, once upon a time cosmopolitan, today a ghost town. Constantinople has retained something of its former charm, but it too has degenerated into a ghost of itself," he kept saying, cursing the plague of nationalism that had converted the blooming cosmopolitan cities of the Mediterranean into pathetic monocultural backwaters. According to Christos P., nationalism was a specific mental disease that had reached those places from the cold, tight-fisted West; it was Europe's incurable sickness that tended to hit small nations, those which, according to him, had been delivered by means of cesarean section from history's womb and which possessed an enfeebled immune system. "We in the Balkans are the orphaned children of three empires, the Roman, Byzantine, and Ottoman," he would say with his eyes glued to the large map of the Balkans including Istanbul that was permanently spread over his hallway's long wall in the apartment. There was a strip of paper on the map on which Christos had inscribed by hand in large letters, "To search for racial purity in the Balkans is like searching for virgins in a whorehouse."

• ■ •

Christos P. was a first cousin of Evangelia's husband (who had died three years ago). Evangelia was the one who called him one day on the telephone and told him in a distressed, anguished voice that she had decided to narrate the slaughterhouse story to some author or journalist, in any case a trustworthy person capable of recording it. Christos P. then locked his two dogs in one of his apartment's bedrooms should their presence be inappropriate for such a meeting, and told her, "I know the ideal person to hear your story." He meant his neighbor Karl.

Evangelia met Karl for the first time several weeks after her oncologist informed her that she had only a few more months to live. She came filled with hesitation to this first meeting, like a young girl from the provinces evasive and unsure regarding her initial encounter with a future husband. But neither her fear nor her suspicion lasted long. Perhaps it was because Christos, in whom she had absolute confidence, had described Karl to her using the very best words, or perhaps because Karl, neither native nor foreign, was "something" she had never encountered in her life — something, in her eyes, that made him the ideal person to listen to her confession.

They met five or six times in Karl's small apartment. After she had exhumed portions of the story from memory, as one lifts the remains of a decaying corpse out of the tomb, she would suddenly stop. "I cannot go further!" she would tell him, turning Sphinx-like into stone. Then, bewildered, she would jump out of her chair as though awakening from sleepwalking and seeing herself at the brink of a cliff. "Everything I've told you, tear it up! This is the last time you'll see me!" she would say to Karl in a manner almost hostile. Yet a few days later she would change her mind, they would meet again, and she would continue her confession. "Promise me you'll publish this only after my funeral," she told him in a commanding tone when she had finished.

Karl kept his word. Two months after Evangelia's funeral he published a portion of her confession on his Facebook page.

"This story will become a book," he wrote at the portion's conclusion.

Karl and my father disagreed sufficiently despite everything else. My father was more devoted to nationality than to communism. He believed simply that communism, better than any other ideology, served our small, poor nation . . . In any case, what I want to report is that my father needed to believe in something — how shall I say it? — something higher, something collective, something that surpassed the individual. He himself always declared: "Without the collective, the individual has no meaning. The individual is an isolated letter while the collective is the entire alphabet." As for

Karl, he was allergic to the word "collective." But how can someone bear the unbearable weight of isolation without feeling that he belongs to something that exceeds the individual's dimensions, something that is eternal, that gives meaning to our inescapable mortality?

•4•

Every nation exhibits "national taboos," so named because they abide deeply buried in the collective forgetfulness of the majority of citizens, committed as they are to "avoidance of truth" (alternatively termed "legislated ignorance" or "status quo"). We might suggest, allowing ourselves a rough analogy, that "legislated ignorance" resembles the inhabitants' incomprehension of their sewage system. Everyone knows that it exists, yet nobody talks about it except when some serious mishap occurs in the system and its disgusting contents flood the city's streets. When "legislated ignorance" is destroyed by meddlers contravening a national taboo, it is therefore as though the sewage system of an entire city has been impaired, exploded into the air. And nothing is worse than when "legislated ignorance" is vexed by a foreigner, a passerby, an Other.

• ■ •

At first, threats and insults reached Karl as messages in his Facebook and email accounts: "filthy Albanian," "ungrateful barbarian," "dirty dog," "snake without a tail," "reptile," "rat," "I'll flay you alive," "go back to your fucking homeland." A few days later his answering machine filled with unknown male voices that repeated the same expressions: "filthy Albanian," "ungrateful barbarian," "dirty dog," "snake without a tail," "reptile," "rat," "I'll flay you alive," "go back to your fucking homeland." Hearing or reading these hate messages, Karl felt a mixture of panic and disgust that completely paralyzed him. He attempted then to sketch in his imagination the facial characteristics of the unknown people who were threatening him. He wondered if they were the usual types like those he met daily in the street: people who went to the dentist when they felt a toothache, who made love or masturbated, who feared solitude, who caressed their children after they returned home early in the evening or late at night?

• ▪ •

He tried to isolate himself from the threats by changing his telephone number and closing his Facebook account. The virtual Facebook window to the world, to which he had paid minimum attention in the past, had provoked the entire mess. He sought consolation from his Greek friends and acquaintances. The majority belonged to the category of people who are described as "progressives" in political jargon — namely, those who in taverna conversations scorned nationalism and declared their sympathy for immigrants in loud voices. Yet precisely now when Karl had such a need for their presence and support, they were avoiding him, especially since the day when an MP of the neo-Nazi political party Golden Dawn had mentioned Karl's name from the podium of the Greek Parliament.

The MP was a youngish, large-bodied man about 35 years old with a shaven head that gleamed like a white sheet just removed from the washing machine. He was known to everyone by the nickname "Adolph of the Rock" owing to lyrics such as *"I'll not allow illegal immigrants to pollute white nations / I'll not allow Jews to ruin us,"* composed by him for the rock band *"This Is Sparta."* On the day he mentioned Karl's name from the parliamentary podium he was wearing a black shirt, black trousers, and a black necktie, while his shaven head seemed like a white lightbulb atop a black pillar. He raised his arms on high, shook his fat neck like a boxer climbing into the ring, puckered his lips in the manner of a three-year-old infant viewing with disgust the meal set in front of him, and shouted, "Karl M, an illegal immigrant from Albania whom we fed, a cruddy Muslim who became a real person in our country but an ungrateful one, a serpent whom we nursed at our bosom, this agent of the Jews who wants the annihilation of the Greek race — he dares to make propaganda for Greater Albania. We nourish and hold to our bosom a hundred thousand snakes like this garbage. The time has come for us to expel them, to clean up our place the way we wipe a toilet with Kleenex!" The other MPs of Golden Dawn who were in the parliament chamber at that moment clapped hysterically, accompanying the thwack of their sweaty palms with whistles, like hooligans. The MPs of the other parties, few in number, remained silently in their seats with drowsy eyes. This speech in parliament by the MP with shaven head was replicated afterwards on the news bulletins of private television stations under titles such as "Albanian Islamists Dream of Greater Albania" or "Albanians Provoke and Raise Claims about the Region of Tsamouria."

From the moment when Karl's name began to circulate on television screens, everything around him radically changed. Friends now did not answer either his telephone calls or the email messages that he sent them. He stopped receiving invitations to mid-afternoon or evening meals. No bookstore organized presentations of his books any longer. Letters from female admirers ceased arriving while hate messages from males filled the inbox of his electronic correspondence. A feeling of abysmal emptiness, which he had almost forgotten, filled Karl's heart, liver, and lungs at this time: *an abysmal feeling that he was foreign and undesirable.*

• ■ •

The only person who continued to knock on Karl's door was Christos P., his neighbor with the two hysterical dogs, precisely the individual who had brought Evangelia into Karl's life. Christos had also knocked on Karl's door on the day when Adolph of the Rock had called Karl a serpent from the rostrum of Parliament. "I saw that fucking Nazi on television," he said, rushing into Karl's apartment. "It's all my fault, Karl, my son," he added. "I'm the one who caused you your troubles."

Christos's carefree, bon vivant countenance now resembled the look of a staring, frightened old man. Tall and thin, he stood in front of Karl as though he were the faithful effigy of Evangelia's father in the slaughterhouse, his wrinkled fingers fumbling in his unshaven goatee like someone seeking a solution. "Karl, leave this country before it's too late," was his advice, his voice sounding as though confessing defeat. At that moment Christos P. seemed to be a metaphor of Greece itself, which was collapsing from the weight of unbearable debts and economic crises — a shadow of himself, aged, resigned, totally unable to protect or console Karl. He was like someone preparing to depart on a mysterious voyage far away from his home and two dogs, far away from the huge map of the Balkans in his apartment's hallway, far away from Athens, from memories of the cities where he had lived, from whatever connected him with himself and others.

PART 4

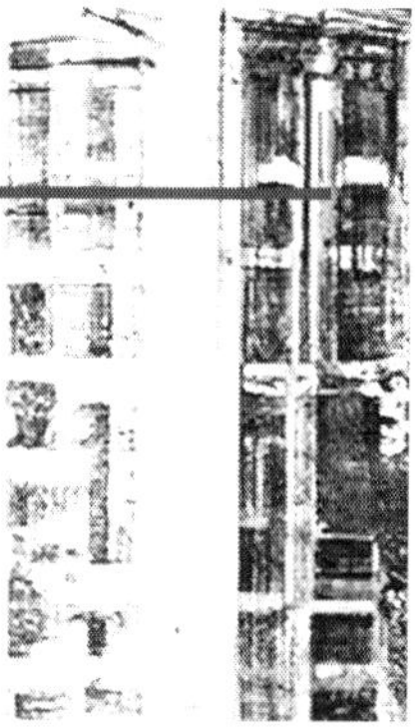

• 1 •

The lives of Fatmira P. and Karl had nothing in common, starting with the fact that Fatmira P. had not even been born in Ters. Exactly how she was born and who brought her into the world remain a mystery. At any rate, we owe to a drunkard the fact that immediately following her birth she did not return to the darkness of nonexistence.

As he was returning home soused to the eyeballs one night in March 1993, the drunkard's eyes fell by chance upon something that resembled a white bundle abandoned in the middle of the village's muddy road. He approached on staggering feet. With a glazed over, dizzied look he discovered that this was not a package but an old woolen blanket inside of which was wrapped an infant. He then began to interrogate himself to make sure that the strange vision in front of him was not an idle fancy of his raki-soaked imagination (a method of self-control that he had also employed in the past). At that very moment the infant began a heartrending wail. Panic overcame the drunkard. He tried to distance himself with quick strides but the child's crying immobilized him. "This was a different kind of bawling, something like a dirge and prayer all together," he used to say afterwards each time he recited in the village café the story of the unknown baby he had found in the middle of the road.

He returned home with the unknown baby in his arms. There the same scene took place every time this man returned intoxicated. His wife, who never slept until her husband appeared on the doorstep, bombarded him at first with curses and then begged him with tearful eyes to abandon "satanic drink." That night, however, when he brought home the heartrending "gift" in addition to his drunken self, the curses terminated on the wife's lips. With fear and astonishment she affixed her gaze upon the old woolen blanket. Her gaping sight met the baby's swollen eyes, which seemed larger than the lamp that threw a weak light into the hall of their poor household. "Take it, wife, 'cause it'll fall out of my arms," said the husband in a bloated voice, his legs staggering. His words sounded like Siri's on a broken Apple iPhone.

"What is this you brought, you good-for-nothing?" the wife managed to sputter in a trembling voice.

When the baby landed in her arms, she froze, rooted to the spot. Her initial fluster quickly granted place, however, to her maternal instinct. Forgetting both curses and husband, she devoted herself to the abandoned infant's care.

Fatmira P.'s body had turned light purple from cold.

• ■ •

In that forgotten village of central Albania where usually nothing happened in any of the seasons of the year, the story of the abandoned infant acquired fairytale dimensions. Various people ventured that the child had been left by the Gypsy family that had passed by two days earlier. Others insisted that the child's mother must be one of the village's unmarried women. "Since the regime fell, women have cut loose," complained several men, grinding their teeth. Still others reached the point of advancing the theory that the baby had been left behind by visitors from another planet, since a month earlier a different intoxicated resident of the village had claimed that around midnight he viewed an extraterrestrial disk landing on the village baker's roof.

Despite such innumerable speculations and fantasies, the abandoned baby was turned over to the police. They delivered it to the nearest hospital and the hospital consigned it to the orphanage of Shkodër, a city in northern Albania. Fatmira P. spent several years there until she was adopted by a fifty-year-old childless couple from Ters. (Rumor has it that the drunkard who found her in the middle of the street had given her the name Fatmira, which in Albanian means "good luck.")

• ■ •

In Ters, where everybody and everything has some nickname, the husband and wife who adopted Fatmira P. were known as "The Mismatched Couple," seeing that the husband, Rustem, was from a Gypsy family. The couple's love affair and especially their marriage had caused quite a stir in Ters. The small city had known many religiously mixed marriages in its history, but a marriage between a Gypsy man and a "white" woman had never been seen. Falma, the young white woman who eloped owing to her love for Rustem, had been renounced forever by her family. The love story of his daughter with a Gypsy was the chief reason, according to gossip, why her father had dropped dead from a stroke two weeks after the daughter's marriage. As for Rustem's family, no one now knew either where they came from or where they had gone.

With the passage of time, the couple managed to win the respect of Ters's inhabitants, which is difficult even for those who have not been stigmatized. (Something similar is confirmed by the well-known saying: "It's harder to win Ters's respect than for the Pope to win Rome's.") However, the couple's dream to have children remained unrealized, a fact that filled their souls with sadness. When both approached the age of 50, they decided to adopt a child from the orphanage. With much effort and ample bribery they adopted Fatmira P. Thus it happened that she too ended up living in Ters with her two adoptive parents in an apartment house across from Karl's.

• ■ •

When Fatmira P. grew up, her impressive beauty became an object of Tersian commentary by both men and women. Favorable and unfavorable conversations about her took place. Many said she was the most beautiful girl in Albania (or, rather, in the entire Balkans). Others, chiefly the men, repeated their well-known clichés – for example, that most beautiful women sooner or later end up as whores. Some, on the other hand, fueled the Tersians' insatiable imaginations with cockeyed scenarios. It was whispered in the cafés of Ters that Fatmira P. was the lover of one of the city's best known Mafiosi, Loni son of Sanije, who had returned to Ters after having roamed for years in Europe selling narcotics and women. There were also those who said that she was a sleepwalker like Lady Macbeth and swore that they had seen her after midnight, when the streets of Ters are empty, crossing the Avenue de l'Europe from side to side dressed in a see-through nightgown. Finally, there are those who disparaged her during the day and contrived poems for her at night. Strange city, Ters, where a person sleeps as a scandalmonger and wakes up as a poet!

All of this shrouded the name of Fatmira P. in a cloak of mystery. Yet, on the other hand, that winter afternoon when the tragic event became known it was as though the Tersians had been struck by lightning. Not even those with the most frenzied of imaginations could have conjectured that Fatmira P. would become the protagonist of such a ghastly story.

• ▪ •

Only when she was discovered dead in the seat of a luxury sedan, next to the lifeless body of her lover, did it become known that Fatmira P. maintained a secret sexual relationship with a man twice her age. Her lover, named Todi Z., was married and the father of two children. He was the wealthiest and most powerful man in Ters, known chiefly by the nickname "Concrete Boss." In his youth, before the regime fell, he was a sergeant in the Albanian army who supervised the cleaning of excrement left in bunkers by passersby. When the regime fell, Todi Z. disappeared into unknown destinations for about a decade. He returned three times heavier, his pockets filled with cash.

It was the period when Ters was dominated by a construction mania. Consistent with rumors (most likely promulgated by Todi Z. himself), one day, standing on top of the old city's hill, he pronounced these words: "I shall become the Concrete Boss." In a few years Todi Z. had indeed eliminated from the game by hook or by crook everyone who asserted the same title. The fame of Todi Z. in any case reached its zenith after the construction of the pair of huge multistory towers at the center of Ters that the inhabitants baptized as the Twin Towers of New York City because Ters was a provincial Balkan city with a huge existential need to see itself as mirroring the world's best-known megalopolis.

• ■ •

The lifeless bodies of the two lovers, discovered a short distance outside of Ters near the concrete factory that belonged to Todi Z., occupied a luxury automobile: a brand-new Jaguar XJ purchased a few weeks before the murder. In the streets of Ters — where for half a century not a single private car had existed because private cars were forbidden by the communists — this was the first time an opulent vehicle of this type (whose seats massaged the backs of its passengers) had circulated. When the discovery was learned by the Tersians, whose imaginations thirsted for such details, the Jaguar XJ of the Concrete Boss became in the minds of the small town's residents something between a fairytale flying carpet and a Batmobile.

Hour after hour I keep asking myself how my life would have been if, like Karl, I had gone far away from Ters. I wonder if I would have loved a foreign woman and married her. I wonder if I would have found work in some European or American hospital and have felt myself respected the same as I do here in Ters. Would I have returned often to Ters or perhaps have forgotten its existence? I wonder if my father would have resisted my departure. Would he have forgiven me or felt betrayed, as he did when Karl departed?

• 2 •

While in cafés and at home the Tersians were becoming immersed in stressful discussions about the macabre event, Karl wandered all by himself through the streets. In his 27 years far away from Ters, he had returned to his native city no more than five or six times. His visits were brief, a few days at most, making his father ask him each time, "Why are you in such a hurry to leave?" This time, however, a strange desire had taken hold of Karl, something resembling the yearning of a person visiting Ters for the first time or the haste of someone wishing to be punctual in every respect for the last time. After having roamed the cobblestones of the old city's alleyways and passed through the squares and pothole-filled streets of the new city, when returning to the family's apartment in the evening Karl would eat the evening meal with Frederik's entire family and, after talking for a short time with them without any special enthusiasm, would politely bid them good night and enclose himself in his room to read and write. While he was shutting the door to his room behind him, Frederik and his wife would stare into each other's eyes as a way of confirming silently the same thought: "Karl is a very strange person."

One morning when Frederik saw Karl leafing through a notebook yellowed with age, he asked him what he had been reading those days.

"Something about Ters's history," Karl answered curtly, indicating that he was not inclined to continue the discussion.

A Brief History of Ters

IDAJET G.

January 1981

CHAPTER 1

Ters is a small Balkan town. Yet its streets, when you wander through them, give you the impression that the town is four times larger than its actual dimensions, perhaps because it is two cities in one. The old city stretches with its stone houses over a hill. If you observe these houses from a distance, they appear like domino pieces supporting each other in a strict and at the same time fragile equilibrium. The old city is divided into three neighborhoods: the Mahalla of the Cross, the Mahalla of Sacrifice, and the Mahalla of the Book. The invisible dividing lines between them used to be houses of worship, all destroyed in 1967, but the names of the districts have nevertheless remained the same.

At the hill's summit, a sort of Acropolis, stands the celebrated Ters Citadel, according to various sources the last in the Balkans that resisted Mehmed the Conqueror. It is said that the Sultan himself, after conquering the Citadel with difficulty, changed the city's name from Gur[5] or Kurrë[6] to the Turkish name Ters. It seems that he was embittered by the fact that

5. Albanian, meaning "stone."

6. Albanian, meaning "never."

the city's inhabitants preferred the Venetians to the Ottomans. After capturing Ters, the sultan gave a command, in retaliation for the pigheadedness of the inhabitants, for half of them to change their religion, either by cajolery or by the whip. That is when "motley families" became apparent in Ters, in which members of the same family belonged to different religions. During daylight the same people prayed in the mosque and the two churches, Orthodox and Catholic, while at dusk they visited the synagogue. "Paradise and politics are like roulette gambling, whereas the hand that wrote holy books is One," they said as they passed from one house of worship to the next. Be that as it may, at the entrance to the Citadel of Ters there still exist today the words of Aşík Paşá Záde, the sultan's personal historian, written on a marble tablet: "All of the conquests of Mehmed the Conqueror were completed with the conquest of Ters."

After the conquest, the city fell into absolute obscurity, as though it had never existed upon earth. (The eminent and powerful Tersians were living now in Constantinople, the capital of the Ottoman Empire, far away from the increasingly impoverished Ters.) The city's obscurity lasted for centuries, at least until the nineteenth, when the famous French romantic poet Lamartine spent a night in one of Ters's caravansaries, resting on his journey to the ancient ruins of Athens. The poet became dumbfounded when he saw that the same people visited the mosque with its blue minaret in the morning, two churches, the Orthodox and the Roman Catholic, at midday, and the small Sephardic synagogue at sundown. He wrote, "The inhabitants of this poverty-stricken place seem to possess a strange gift: they fail where most Europeans succeed and they succeed where most Europeans have failed." After that brief report, Ters fell once again into oblivion.

It reappeared in bureaucratic reports from Europe's Great Powers, in a minimum number of ethnological studies and a great number of patriotic poems, as soon as the city, with not even its own inhabitants understanding how, entered the agitated age of nationalism when the Ottoman Empire began to shed its dependencies like a corncob losing its kernels. That period did not bring any special change regarding the architecture of Ters. The city continued to exist with its three mahallades on top of the hill, with houses that resembled people afraid of solitude, cramming one against the next. On the hilltop stood the Citadel of Ters like a lonely, senescent despot; at the bottom of the hill flowed the Skamandros River, which the inhabitants of Ters, after Albania's independence from the Ottoman Empire (that almost unbelievable achievement!), began to call La Seine. It was the time when the Tersians stopped looking toward Istanbul and started looking with expectation toward Paris. The new nationalists interpreted the river at the bottom of the hill as a good sign. "All the wealthy and powerful cities of Europe are built around a river," they kept asserting with hope (the kind that finally expires) as they enumerated with childish enthusiasm those crossed by some river — Paris, Berlin, Rome, Vienna, Saint Petersburg, London — cities in which the history of Europe and humankind was written.

Changing the name of the Skamandros to La Seine did not save the Tersians from the horrors brought by World War I. In the winter of 1915 the first foreign soldiers set foot upon the city's cobblestones. They were Serbian. It would be difficult, however, to call them conquerors. They reached Ters dressed in rags and half-fainting from hunger, tearfully begging the inhabitants for a share of pumpkin pita. Hunted down by the army of Frederik the Great, these Serbian soldiers had crossed the almost impassable Albanian Alps heading for Corfu, where the Italian fleet was waiting to save them. King Peter I of Serbia, riding a horse all skin and bones that looked more like a stallion's ghost, reached Ters half-dead. Two elderly Tersian healers massaged the king's numb body for hours with raki. When he finally opened his eyes he gazed around with surprise and asked, *"Koji je ovaj grad?"*[7] That is why in his personal journal the city of Ters appears with the name Tersograd.

During all those troubled years, one also finds Ters under the name Tersoupolis. The reason is that in the spring of 1916, when

7. Serbian: "Which city is this?"

violets and roses were blossoming in Ters's gardens, two battalions of Greek paramilitaries (the so-called "sacred irregulars") occupied the city. As soon as they set foot in Ters they began a campaign to Hellenize everything dead and alive. But on October 2, 1916, when the paramilitaries had already controlled the city for a full six months, French forces invaded Ters (the French army remained known in Ters as "the Arab army" because half of the French soldiers came from the French colonies in North Africa). "I give you a twenty-four-hour deadline to withdraw," the head of the French forces, Colonel Descoins, telegraphed the Greek paramilitaries. At first the Greeks maintained that they desired to keep Ters as a colony, as the French had kept Casablanca or Algeria. Let alone that six months earlier the city's inhabitants had themselves changed the name to Tersoupolis. Colonel Descoins, well known for his belligerent and haughty character, said to the leader of the Greek paramilitaries with a belittling wave of the hand, *"À Ters, l'État c'est moi!"*[8] The paramilitaries, being fewer in number and poorly armed compared to the French soldiers, withdrew, cursing Descoins's mother.

From October 1916 until the end of World War I the French declared Ters an independent

8. "In Ters, I am the state." "L'État c'est moi" is a quotation attributed to the French King Louis XIV. It is used in reference to someone who claims absolute power without boundaries or rivalries.

democracy. Its official name was République Balkanique de Ters. That is why, still today in Ters, the most widespread language after Albanian is French. On the day the French withdrew from Ters, the clownish Colonel Descoins wrote in his journal: "Except for the fact that nature's most hateful creatures, mosquitoes, thrive here, Ters is an interesting city. Its inhabitants remind me of Homeric heroes. For certain hours on end they resemble that man in his dotage in the *Iliad*, Priam, and for other hours on end they resemble the lotus eaters in the *Odyssey*."

CHAPTER 2

As for the new or modern Ters, it was built more or less in the decade of the 1930s on the river's other bank, directly opposite the old city, upon a surface that the Tersians named "Desert" because the expanse of soil strewn with white pebbles is as completely level as the palm of an adolescent boy's hand. These were the years when Zog I reigned in Albania, the king who spoke German better than Albanian since he had spent his youth as a lieutenant in the Austro-Hungarian army. King Zog I came so close to Benito Mussolini's fascist Italy that the latter needed only to yawn in order to guzzle down once and for all that small noisy place filled with hills, rushing streams, mountains, and mosquitoes.

One morning Italian architects suddenly appeared in Ters. They were looking for an unspoiled tract on which to build a fascistic architectural utopia. Ters charmed them, perhaps owing to its great age or excellent climate. But mostly they were extremely curious to see how the town's old-time residents would react when the new city germinated in front of their eyes. From that moment onward Ters was transformed into a worksite, an experimental center for the diverse utopias that paraded through Europe after World War I.

The new city was planned to be the opposite of the old one, without the narrow, crooked, cobblestoned alleyways that resembled the labyrinth of Daedalus, or the stone houses leaning against each other like performers in a Greek *tsámikos* dance. Predominant in the new city would be avenues completely straight as though drawn with a ruler, buildings with majestic façades, marble columns like haughty phalluses rising toward heaven in the public squares, which in turn resembled enormous cenotaphs.

The inhabitants of Ters's old city on the hill were stupefied as they monitored the construction of the new city on the Desert. Several, especially among the elderly, said the new city had nonrealistic dimensions and was built with the aim of forcing the servants of God to realize their absolute nothingness by comparison. On the other hand, youthful inhabitants who had begun to be educated in the West wove praises for the new city in verse or wild choric odes. It was the city of the future, they bellowed vehemently, the city of cities!

A silent war then broke out between the unified twin cities. Despite everything, the scales of history were clearly weighted toward the new Ters, where almost all the important buildings of governmental management and bureaucracy were built; the Town Hall, Ministerial District, police department, hospital and maternity clinics, post office, plus modern pubs, movie houses of the type where films would display modern women and also automobiles (which made the old city appear ten times more pathetic), a new football stadium, the Opera House, railway station, Slaughterhouse Bossio (named for its Italian architect, Gerardo Bossio) next to the new cemetery of Ters, the town's library, bookstore, two printing shops, the high school, MAPO Fashions selling stylish Italian clothing, the House of Fasho, a Dopolavoro club franchise, and the prison cells where political prisoners were tortured with castor oil.

Street names made the two cities' differences even more prominent. The old city still retained former names such as Path of the Lost Horse or Nun's Neck. Streets of the new city bore pompous names such as Avenue de l'Empire Romain or Avenue des Colonies.

The new city's inhabitants had less and less need for the old city. Remaining there now were only the former undertakers' establishments, the bakeries, two Turkish baths, cafés with hookahs where gray-haired men related old stories of epic hospitality or revenge, recollecting or sprucing up moments from their lives at some point in Istanbul, Thessaloniki, Bucharest, Alexandria, or Beirut.

Young inhabitants of the new city no longer felt any need to pray in the mosques, churches, or synagogue of old Ters, believing that they belonged to a new epoch that promised once and for all to leave the past behind. They performed gymnastics every morning to keep their tummies from resembling round barrels like their fathers' tummies;

they took pills to avoid constipation; they imagined a hierarchical, well-disciplined society with ultraclean streets and exemplary genes. Intoxicated by feelings of superiority, they viewed whoever disagreed with their *Weltanschauung* as humanly redundant.

Compassion, they held, is a disease of the vanquished.

In a few years, the new Ters made the old Ters resemble a relic from the past. The two cities became equal again only during World War II, specifically when the Italian conquerors were replaced by the German Wehrmacht (about whom it was difficult for anyone to ascertain whether they marched with open or closed eyes). The famine that crushed the city, both the stone part on the hill and the new part on the Desert, brought everyone close together. Struggling to keep alive, inhabitants of the two-cities-in-one began to speak to each other without any teasing or sarcasm; they took pride in exchanging provisions, clothes, medicines, homemade pasta for Roman sugar, duck meat for the underwear of British secret agents, beef tripe for quinine to fight malaria.

Toward the end of November 1944, after fighting a German brigade in a cruel battle that destroyed the Great Square almost entirely, Albanian partisans entered Ters as liberators. The inhabitants, exhausted from famine, regarded them with thankfulness but also suspicion. The Catholic archbishop of Ters,

Don Pulbardha, described these communists as a squalid theatrical troupe with long rifles and ravenous glances (later, he paid for those words with his life). However, the majority of the Tersians did not know what to think of the city's new conquerors.

They simply waited.

While waiting, they gathered up the corpses of 28 of their fellow Tersians who had been executed in the courtyard of Slaughterhouse Bossio, their bodies already torn to pieces by famished dogs. This was the Germans' retaliation for the Tersians' refusal to hand over the Jews who found refuge in the city's dungeons and cellars — not only local Jews but also those who had come from the Balkans and Western Europe hoping to save their skins in this place in the middle of nowhere.

All the inhabitants were ordered after the funerals and burials to assemble in Ters's Great Square, where the Eternal and Unmistakable Leader of the communists would give a speech.

They went with their stomachs rumbling from hunger and curiosity. It was cold and drizzling.

Neither roses nor violets had blossomed in Ters that year.

The Great Leader of the communists was a tall, presentable man who continually waved his index finger at the crowd as he spoke. He resembled those youths of the city who said they belonged to a new age in which the true history of mankind was beginning. In any case, his manner of speaking reminded one of children inflating balloons, since issuing from his mouth came formidable declarations such as "Ters's future will be communistic and bright," and "Thanks to the glorious struggle of our partisans, Albania belongs at last to Albanians." The Tersians listening to him held their breath like experienced divers plunging to the sea bottom. They did not know whether they should be pleased or terrified. There were some, especially the younger ones, who believed what they heard. "Look around you," they said, pointing to the ruined houses that the Germans had burned. "Worse cannot happen, brothers. Things can only get better. At least these are our own people."

But one week after the speech by the Unmistakable Leader, the famous fortune teller of Ters, Meti the Blind, who lived in Melancholy Street, said something that left the Tersians in a hopeless tangle. "Deep darkness departed. Deep darkness arrived," he announced as though from the Delphic Oracle. Such disturbance was aroused in the Tersians' minds and hearts that the communists were forced to apply urgent measures as a way of forestalling disturbances. At midday in front of everyone's wide-open eyes, a partisan patrol violently dragged Meti the Blind away as though he were a sheep being led to slaughter. They took him alive and returned him dead. They planted the body afterwards in the Great Square, not lying on the ground, however, as is determined by unwritten laws for every corpse, whether friend or foe. They tied him with rope to one of the still-standing Roman-style columns built by the fascist Italian architects, the ones resembling phalluses raised toward heaven. The corpse now resembled a scarecrow used to frighten ravens. On its neck they hung a piece of cardboard proclaiming "Freedom for the people; death for traitors."

All the Tersians, young and old, men and women, those missing half the teeth in their mouths and those with golden teeth, gossipers and those who failed to talk even while asleep, pregnant women and virgins — all received a command to go to the Great Square for the purpose of spitting on Meti the Blind's corpse. The few residents who abstained were arrested on the spot and executed on the same day, without a trial. They were placed against the white wall of the old city's brothel (today's cheese pie shop, its wall now known as the "Wall of Tears"). The remaining residents of Ters saw with frightened eyes the red blood that splattered the brothel's white wall like the frenzied brushstrokes of a painter of abstract art. A few determined then to take to their heels, cross the border, flee to wherever their legs could carry them. It was learned like greased lightning, however, that the borders had been hermetically sealed. Consequently, these few returned and, with lips trembling from fright and disgust, went to the Great Square with all the others to toss their spittle upon Meti the Blind's corpse.

That evening, wrapped in darkness inside their homes, the Tersians prayed to God with tearful eyes to be forgiven. Two of them, the grandson of the former governor of Lebanon and the owner of Slaughterhouse Bossio, committed suicide. The two best-known poets of Ters, Shterg P. and Kadri S., followed entirely opposite courses. The first decided not to write a single word for as long as the new conquerors remained in power (he died alone and forgotten, without having written anything for 45 years); the second, under candlelight that very evening, began his epic poem: "Leader, where can I discover your heroic roots?" Rabbi Moïse, his fingers deformed by arthritis, entered in his notebook, "Ters is a city in which European history has lost its footing, fallen down, and broken its neck."

At dawn the next day, the communist governor of Ters, Mehmet S., sent a brief telegram to the Great Leader, that presentable man who a week earlier had spoken in Ters's Great Square: "Public spitting on traitor M. T. completed absolute success STOP 95% population enthusiastic participation STOP 5% resisters neutralized pronto STOP 2 smidges suicide STOP."

No one knows, even today, where the corpses of Meti the Blind, the inhabitants who were executed, and the two who committed suicide may be found . . .

There are moments when I understand Karl and the others who departed from Ters and went far away. There are moments when Ters chokes one, frightens one. The cadavers on which I perform an autopsy are often people who died senselessly, one killing another over a conversation or a bit of fencing. . . . Sometimes I go to church after the autopsies and pray to God for myself, for others, for Ters . . . On the other hand, however, I think that it's the same everywhere in the world, even in the richer places. Yesterday I saw a documentary on Chicago, how much violence exists there and how many crimes occur. Despite all that, the residents continue to lead their lives nicely enough. If you are a normal person, there is no reason for you to be touched by the evil happening around you. That was my philosophy yesterday and still is today: to keep seeing what is good and positive. At bottom, the majority of Tersians live normal lives with their worries, families, dreams. They go to work, make love, get married, have children, the children go to school. We often join our group of friends for the midday meal or a little something in the evening; we talk over coffee, drink the world's best raki, go to movies, theater, our wives are amazing cooks, we men argue over football, say how lucky we are to enjoy such a good climate, go to the seashore in summertime and, if some misfortune happens, each of us finds himself near someone else, much nearer than people do in Chicago, New York, or Berlin . . .

• 3 •

Frederik in his medical whites stood in front of the lifeless bodies of Fatmira P. and Todi Z. Both were lying side by side now in the morgue like two ghosts, naked beneath the autopsy's white sheets, her hair long, his scalp bald, and with a label hanging from the thumb of each: first name, last name, date of death, cadaver number.

Next to Frederik stood the police chief, about 40 years old, moderate height, firmly built, slightly enlarged middle, with an old scar apparently from a knife wound above his right eyebrow. Next to the chief was a young policeman with a blue notebook in hand.

"Well, professor, what does science tell us?" the chief asked Frederik with the ease of someone wishing to show that he had everything under control despite the difficult state of affairs.

Frederik remained silent for a moment. Still wearing autopsy gloves, he crossed his hands and said with puckered lips:

"Science tells us that Todi killed Fatmira and then killed himself."

"Understood," said the chief of police. Neither spoke for a moment.

The young policeman entered something in his notebook.

"But it doesn't end there," added Frederik.

The chief gave him a surprised look.

"Fatmira was carrying a fetus in her body. It appears that the child was Todi's. Probably that was why he decided to get rid of her," Frederik said, his eyes fixed on the two cadavers.

"Unbelievable," said the chief, his hand touching the old scar above his eyebrow. "So why did he kill himself then?" he asked Frederik.

Frederik shrugged his shoulders as though wanting to say, "That surpasses my competence."

"Give us your expertise with your signature, professor," the chief then said as he withdrew a pack of cigarettes from his jacket pocket.

Once more, the young policeman entered something in his notebook.

As Frederik covered the cadavers again, the chief kept watching him, imagining the two lifeless bodies entering, separately, the "white mouths," as he termed the freezers that prevented cadavers from decomposing.

The chief's job brought him unavoidably into contact with cadavers, many of which were in advanced stages of decomposition. The first time this happened, about ten years earlier, he kept leaping out of bed at night for several weeks, perturbed, covered with sweat. For quite a long time the stench of decomposing corpses remained pasted inside his nose like a magnet upon a metallic surface. From then onward he would view his fellow human beings differently when they were alive. One could say that he felt slightly more sympathy for them. Everything that people invent and accomplish, he thought, starting with perfumes and fancy clothes like Fatmira P.'s dress on the day of her murder, and leading to the children they bring into the world — everything is a shield to protect themselves from the ubiquitous presence of loss, is an attempt to cajole death.

"Professor, do you believe the soul continues to live after death?" the chief suddenly asked Frederik.

It was Frederik's turn to be surprised this time.

"For some people it's good that nothing exists after death," he answered, looking into his interlocutor's eyes.

"Let's go outside to smoke a cigarette. It's hard to stay inside any longer," said the chief, glancing for the last time around the morgue.

They went outside without conversing.

Remaining silent, the three of them smoked in the hospital's small garden, their eyes fixed upon the trees' bare limbs.

● ■ ●

"Whores destroy families" and "Whores kill" were the initial slogans that appeared on Ters's walls. The first was written in large red letters on the wall of the building where Fatmira P. had lived; the other, in equally large letters and the same red paint, was on the wall of the Town Hall, near the Great Square.

Spreading pell-mell in Ters was a faulty version of the murder, thanks chiefly to the Concrete Boss's minions who controlled not only the city's builders, its shops that offered games of chance, the local television station and newspaper, Ters Times, but also its Facebook trolls. People in Ters had recently acquired an addiction to virtual reality. It was precisely those trolls who, a few hours after the murder, spread word that it was she, Fatmira P., who murdered Todi Z. and then committed suicide. The next day, when inhabitants were informed by Ters Times that Fatmira P. was carrying a fetus in her womb, the terror they had felt at first concerning the macabre end of the two lovers was transformed into an avalanche of accusations against her. She was now considered the murderer of two people: one alive and another not yet born.

The cafés and homes of Ters were flooded with deep, intense conversations about the two deceased lovers. Yet at the end of each conversation the weight of responsibility fell on Fatmira P. "The old-timers used to say 'Watch out for fires and whores'," uttered someone in the Vieux Fani bar on the Avenue de l'Europe, picking his teeth with his fingernail. "She employed the baby to blackmail Todi," interrupted someone else, next to him, swallowing yet another glass of black Fernet. People did exist, although truly few, who attempted to restore logic and the genuine order of events: that the pistol of the double murder belonged to Todi Z., that he had killed Fatmira P. and had afterwards committed suicide. But the voices of these few were covered over by the picking of teeth and by cursing.

Thus, amid the feverish discussions, maledictions, and misinformation, it happened that both the new and old cities were overwhelmed by a mania for revenge against Fatmira P. Ters decided something never before heard of in its history: to boycott her funeral. Twilight came, church bells filled Ters's atmosphere with the sound of a mournful melody, and the muezzin sang his prayer from the white minaret while Bim the shoemaker declared, "There's a first time for everything."

I've been thinking: Once upon a time things were unambiguous. Women were women and men were men; hierarchy existed, order existed; humans knew who they were and what they desired. Afterward came this new age (as it is called), the age in which everything is higgledy-piggledy, the women not knowing any longer what they want and the men not knowing any longer what they are doing. Recently, two days before the corpses of Todi and the ill-fated female were found, a handful of perverts arrived here from Tirana and organized a demonstration in the Great Square. "We are gay and lesbian," they squeaked, waving those colored flags of theirs that resemble grandmothers' underwear. Who the devil asked you what you are? Keep that to yourselves! No, they tell us: people are at liberty to be and do what they want in public. These theories strike me as utterly ridiculous. Behind what they call "limitless freedom" is hidden a great deception. Only people like Todi who are rolling in money can do as they please. But these rich ones are the minority; the non-rich are and will always be the great majority. In the world of uncontrolled freedom, the majority are imposed upon by the minority: the Jewish banker, the Freemason, the undocumented Mafioso, the gay man with his wallet filled with money from Soros, who wants to make my own son gay because, according to these people, that is the truly genuine freedom.

Salvation from this fraud is the return to strong identity and nationalism. Nationalism is not hatred of others; it is self-love, love for your language, your nation, your race. Nationalism is discipline, hierarchy, order, respect for human nature. It is the fire that will cleanse pollution, the strong leader who will make this crooked cosmos straight.

•4•

Having roamed the streets of Ters, Karl was on his way home as the sun was setting when he caught sight of the wall of an apartment building across the way. He stared for a moment at the slogan on it: "Whores destroy families" in large red letters. These oversized crooked letters were written quickly with faulty spelling. Except for the slogan, everything else was old. Prevailing during those evening hours was a silence frequently interrupted only by some loud voice speaking on the telephone or by some infant wailing.

Slowly, he climbed the stairs of his own apartment building.

No one was home. Turning on the kitchen light, he saw on the large table two plates covered with white napkins. It was his evening meal. Frederik's wife cooked every day for him. Karl felt grateful to his sister-in-law but he also regretted being so reticent and distant all these days. He found a short note on one of the plates. Karl recognized the writing as Frederik's: "We will return late tonight. Hugs."

Going from the kitchen to the sitting room, he sat down in one of its large armchairs. His feet felt heavy and tired. A warm bath will bring me round, he thought. This was the first time since his arrival in Ters that he was at home by himself. He thought that his life in that home could be divided into two parts: happy childhood years and difficult adolescent years. Sinking into the armchair, he closed his eyes.

• ■ •

He saw himself on the stage of his favorite theater, the Emerson Cutler Majestic in Boston. Inarticulate shouts kept issuing from the auditorium which, buried in thick darkness, was blocked from his sight. He could distinguish nothing, not even the small red-colored boxes resembling confessional stalls in Roman Catholic churches, nor the marvelous Beaux Arts décor. Issuing continually from the darkness was only a buzz that sounded like a vacuum cleaner. After a little, however, the inarticulate purr changed into a rhythmical slogan. Karl pricked up his ears to hear:

"Build that Wall"
"Build that Wall"
"Build that Wall"
"Build that Wall"
"Build that Wall"

Feeling overcome by fear, he then plugged his ears with wax. "It's like Odysseus's sailors approaching the Sirens' isle," he thought with satisfaction, as though he had just invented something unimaginably important. The buzz decreased. He removed the wax from his ears. Yet the same rhythmic slogan continued to arrive from the auditorium's darkness:

"Build that Wall"
"Build that Wall"
"Build that Wall"
"Build that Wall"
"Build that Wall"

"Stop! Stop!" screamed Karl with all the strength he possessed.

To his surprise, absolute silence followed.

Then, like an actor on stage, he began to emit from his mouth various formulations unrelated to each other, like those he wrote in his notebook after the election of Trump — formulations he usually read to Klodi.

"People can live very well without sex but cannot live without scapegoats."

Invisible voices then began to scream sarcastically. Karl felt he was a laughingstock, as though standing naked on stage.

"Don't let it touch you, not at all," he then told himself to regain his self-confidence. "From the moment you continue to write, it means you exist."

"How did you meet Klodi? Tell us!" sounded suddenly at that point from a harsh female voice in the theater's dark auditorium.

As though he had been expecting that moment, Karl began to narrate this history.

"It was many years ago, in Tirana, the night when the dictator's statue came down. Klodi found the shoe I had lost in the *mêlée*. The next day she did not come to meet me; she disappeared, having precipitously departed to Israel with her mother. While I was living in Athens, she married a Russian-Jewish astronomer there. They emigrated afterwards to Boston, where she gave birth to two children. For 22 years Klodi and I knew nothing about each other's existence. Later, I saw her one day by chance in a café at the center of Athens, near Constitution Square. She was sitting by herself at a table, like an alienated woman painted by Edward Hopper. Although she was wearing a lovely hat that hid her black hair, I recognized her as someone recognizes his own past, and she recognized me too.

I approached her.

"'Unbelievable,' whispered Klodi.

"'Unbelievable,' I whispered.

"When we met in Athens, Klodi was embarking to Europe on a difficult journey, trying to forget, to escape. She had separated from her husband six months earlier. The moment when she and I found each other again, I was terrified and wanted to leave Greece as soon as possible. Klodi's gaze upon me after so many years made me thirst to repeat a journey that had ended at some point before ever beginning. We set out then from the start, clinging to each other's body with all the attraction of sexual pleasure, all the strength of hope and hopelessness, like survivors clinging to a life-saving dinghy in the ocean's middle.

"The sequel is somewhat complicated," Karl said bluntly, and fell silent.

A hush prevailed in the dark auditorium.

Suddenly a female silhouette emerged from the gloom and approached him slowly, imperceptibly on the steps at stage-side. In her hands she held a world map. Karl recognized his mother. She was smiling. Her fingers were not disabled; her lips were painted red with lipstick. She said nothing, just smiled. Karl, too, began to smile. He felt her fingers and soft palm upon his face, caressing him.

"Darling!" she whispered, her gaze turning melancholic.

Suddenly Karl felt guilt for not sending her a single letter for such a long time, for not even informing her that he was living with Klodi in America. In such a letter he would also have written about other things he had come to understand since leaving Ters — such as, for example: freedom often hurts more than loneliness, and the strangest love is born from pain and desperation.

His mother suddenly asked if he were happy in America.

"I am happy with Klodi," Karl replied with a sort of uncertainty in his voice. "We get along despite some financial difficulties. But," he added, "Klodi always tells me that I should go where people love me." Then he thought to read to his mother the first paragraph of the opening chapter of his new book, *A Short History of Ters.*

His mother extended her hand and clasped Karl's hand, as when he was a small child and she used to hold him by the hand and go to the Great Square to take black and white photographs.

"Let's go home, *biri im*,"[9] she said to him, half in English, half in Albanian.

"Where is home, ma?" Karl asked her in English.

"Don't you feel at home here?" he was asked in English in the same interrogatory tone by the female voice that had inquired how he came to know Klodi.

"Of course I feel at home here. This is my home," answered Karl again in English in a voice that trembled with annoyance.

9. Let's go home, my son.

He turned his head to see his mother. She was no longer there, having receded again into the darkness.

"Ma, don't go away so quickly!" he shouted in Greek, trying to descend from the stage so he could walk toward the dark auditorium.

Although he had no sense of his body's weight, he found he could not move. His feet disobeyed his wish.

Opening his eyes at that moment, he sprang erect as though wishing to confirm that he was no longer dreaming. He looked everywhere, bleary-eyed. The dream had been so realistic that for a moment he believed he had been truly visited by his mother's ghost.

Without eating or bathing, he fell asleep.

• ▪ •

"I'm going to Fatmira's funeral," said Karl, adding, "This city mistreats women even when they're dead."

Frederik, attempting to treat his brother gently, kindly requested him to change his mind. He tried to explain that he himself did not agree with boycotting the funeral. But Karl should strive to understand the Tersians as honest people who make mistakes. He should understand how they live and think, the reasons why they have grown afraid and are exasperated by the murder.

"When all is said and done, isn't this the nature of democracy: the wish of the majority even when the majority is wrong?" asked Frederik with a slight smile, attempting to remain as calm as possible.

Nevertheless, the more Frederik endeavored to make Karl change his mind, the more Karl's obstinacy increased.

"Stop talking about it, Frederik," Karl said. "I have made up my mind."

The two brothers remained standing in the wide corridor next to the large library. It was almost 11 a.m. Sunshine, entering through the sitting room window, illuminated the corridor in part, giving it a prevailing half-light or semidarkness.

Frederik thought to himself that Karl had remained identically the same, that wherever he saw a wall in front of him he would go bash it in with his head.

The expression on Frederik's face changed in the way that someone who has lost patience changes expression. All those days he had done everything to come closer to Karl. He and his wife had looked after him with the greatest generosity. Yet behold the result: Karl once again had proved himself ungrateful.

"Karl, why are you doing this?" asked Frederik with hands trembling now from turmoil. Then, in a quivering voice owing to anger: "Tomorrow you will leave. I'll be here in this same city. Tomorrow you will not be in Ters for everyone to scowl at you. Everyone will scowl at me, at my son, my wife . . . tomorrow, the day after tomorrow, every day! So if you want to do something brave, OK, go to the funeral of that . . . unfortunate. But then do not climb aboard an airplane and disappear somewhere at the end of the world. Stay here, together with me and the others."

Karl looked at Frederik as though he was at his wits' end.

Frederik continued: "If people such as me did not exist, and our father and those poor souls who decided to boycott the funeral, this city would have been wiped out, our nation would have died. As for you, from the day you departed 27 years ago, maybe you returned to Ters three or four times, but every time you came you very quickly asserted, 'I'm leaving,' instead of 'here I am'."

Karl remained silent for a moment, closing his eyes as though endeavoring to exorcise some nightmare. He took a deep breath, then began to speak slowly, like someone attempting to extract an old ghost from memory.

"Do you remember Idajet, our music teacher in high school? Do you remember when they arrested him because one of the students accused him of praising jazz music in class? Our father was then the high school principal. The two of us were sitting in the schoolyard when we saw Idajet wearing handcuffs. He looked like someone they had mistreated. That cheerful, stylish person resembled at that moment a grotesque scarecrow. Idajet in handcuffs, a policeman to his left, our father to his right. Father said, 'This man here is an enemy of the nation and the Party. He wants to corrupt the young generation.' He then called upon all the school's students to spit on Idajet. 'Let's go,' you said, full of enthusiasm, as though we were going to a picnic. Full of anger, I looked at you but did not say anything. I departed stealthily like someone breaking out of prison. You went with the crowd to spit on Idajet. That evening at home a big argument broke out between Father and me. Father called me a deserter and coward. You kept quiet, never said a word. From that day onward the students secretly pasted little slips of paper onto our school bags with 'Son of a fink' written on them. You went tearfully to Father, begging him to find the louts who pasted the slips of paper on us. I wanted to die from shame, wanted the earth to open at that moment and swallow me. That is why I come so seldom to Ters and stay so briefly. I'm afraid I might encounter Idajet in the street or see my former schoolmates, still afraid someone might paste a slip of paper on my back: 'Son of a fink'. . . These days I learned that Idajet has died. I'm sorry that I never found the courage to beg his forgiveness while he was alive. I've also found something else these days: in the room where I sleep, in the bedside table where father kept his diary, a notebook, but Idajet's, not father's. He had begun to write a book . . . I've been reading and re-reading this notebook these days . . . Father not only stole Idajet's life; he wanted also to steal his ideas."

"Are you finished?" asked Frederik. His face had turned ashen.

"Karl, even now you are still taking revenge on Father, and on me. The past is past, with its virtues and defects. Normal people forget the defects and retain the virtues. Normal people do not rummage in bedside tables but stand next to their father in his dying moment . . . You do not belong to the category of normal people . . . That's why Father went to the mosque, to seek pardon for his mistakes. As we say in Ters, 'The forgiven head is not beheaded.' Anyhow, whatever happened in this family happened. But Father never abandoned us, never ceased loving you even though you abandoned him . . . You left when many people were leaving. Father and I stayed here in Ters, went against the many, remained here in this poor spot, keeping each other alive, remained here also in 1996 when the state and everything else was falling apart, when people were shooting each other just to pass the time, when Ters was transformed into a jungle and in the Great Square the various gangs played ball with detached human heads, when a person went to the old market to buy macaroni and was given a pistol for change. Where were you then, Karl? Where were you? You, the rebel, you who burn more for an unknown whore than for your own family. I'll tell you what you are, Karl. You are an arrogant snob, a megalomaniac, an ungrateful elitist, a good-for-nothing traitor!"

Frederik left the house at once, vigorously banging the door behind him.

•5•

The open coffin containing Fatmira P.'s body was in the sitting room of her apartment. Her white face, looked after most likely by her mother, resembled that of a bride preparing to leave her family home. Her head with its black hair was immersed in a pool of red and white rose-petals covering it as far down as the temples in order to hide the scar from the bullet in her skull. Karl, seated next to the coffin, was drinking coffee with her two parents, Rustem and Falma. Their apartment was on the fourth floor. Through the sitting room's translucent curtains one could distinguish the Concrete Boss's Twin Towers.

When Karl was about to enter their home, Fatmira P.'s parents thought he had made a mistake about which door he wanted. All three of them stood silently for a few moments in the corridor. But when Karl said, "I have come to offer my condolences," the parents smiled as though someone had brought them joyful news. "Thank you, thank you," they both exclaimed, trying to keep calm. Their eyes were fatigued; their gestures resembled those of people who feel guilty of something. Karl thought to himself that here was the essence of Ters: the guilty never repent while the innocent always feel guilty.

Seated together in the sitting room, Karl and Fatmira's two parents engaged in a conversation with extended silences. The parents expressed their condolences for Karl's father. They asked him if he had made himself sufficiently comfortable in America. Karl answered mostly in single words, trying to hide any annoyance in his voice. He understood from the parents' look that his unexpected presence had surprised and troubled them. When silence dominated again, Karl said, "I am terribly sorry that you lost your daughter . . . May God grant you strength to endure the pain."

Falma, Fatmira P.'s mother, had begun silently to weep when a light knock was heard on the door. Both parents, rising quickly, went out into the corridor. Karl managed to hear the sound of voices reaching the sitting room but could not comprehend what was being said. Soon the room containing the coffin was entered by Crazy Pandi. Karl had never before seen him dressed in a suit. Attempting to hold his stooped body as straight as possible, he grasped in his right hand an elegant wooden cane while on his bald head he was wearing a black homburg. He extended his trembling hand to Karl and sat down in the chair next to him.

Karl threw a quick glance at the sitting room. The furniture was the same as during the communist period, a specific fashion that existed in all the former communist countries from Poland as far as Cuba, with similar appearance, the same dreary color: an indefinable shade of coffee-brown found in household kitchens and bedrooms, also in interrogators' offices.

He saw two photos of Fatmira P. hanging on the wall above the open coffin. In one she was a small laughing child between her two parents, who were holding her hand. In the other she was alone with dark backcombed hair, her playful intelligent

eyes flirting with the camera. It must have been taken just a few months before she died. Karl silently repeated the verses he had written after his accidental meeting with Kleio in Athens:
po të vije si një mëkat / If you came like a sin
do të prisja si një falje / I would meet you as a pardon
po të vije aq e trishtë si një rrenojë / If you came so sad like a ruin
do të prisja si një strehë / I would meet you as a shelter.

• ▪ •

At the same time that the Concrete Boss's mortal remains were being displayed for public bowing in the large assembly room of Ters's Town Hall, Fatmira P.'s coffin was being prepared for its journey to the cemetery. Her father, Karl, Crazy Pandi, and the driver of the hearse brought the coffin down from the fourth floor with difficulty, halting at each floor so that Crazy Pandi could catch his breath.

When they placed the coffin in the hearse, Fatmira's mother laid a bouquet with white roses on the black wooden cover. The driver asked if he should start; the two parents nodded affirmatively. Her father, Rustem, had requested the driver to proceed along the Avenue de l'Europe at unhurried speed. All four began to follow the hearse with slow steps. It was a cold, sunny February afternoon and the streets of Ters were almost empty. One noticed some passerby turning his head discreetly every so often while he walked, so that he might glimpse the hearse and the few people following it. Several inhabitants had emerged onto their balconies to watch; others observed through their windows, their faces hidden behind thick curtains.

The cemetery was located between Slaughterhouse Bossio and the Mahalla of the Damned. Slaughterhouse was now a ruined, abandoned building resembling a bull's slashed mouth. It was a place where Ters's stray dogs and cats usually found refuge (sometimes together with secret lovers who could discover no other location to have intercourse). As for the Mahalla of the Damned, which had been built roughly in the decade of the 1950s, the regime's "internal enemies," banished to Ters from various parts of Albania, lived in its sheet-metal shanties. Gathered there were bodies, souls, and minds belonging to a category of humanity that the Tersians described as "widely traveled" because most of the inhabitants of the Mahalla of the Damned had studied sometime either elsewhere in Europe or in America. A rumor circulated that in this hell on earth more languages were spoken — around thirty, both dead and alive — than in any other European civilized area. In these sheet-metal shacks resembling cages for wild animals, three (at least) distinguished translators had recently given up the ghost: the translator of Dante, the translator of Djalâl ad-Dîn Rûmî, and Tower of Babel, proficient in 20 languages, translator of Shakespeare and Cervantes, among others. When the Mahalla of the Damned began to be built, the Tersians understood that, above and beyond its role as a place of punishment for those who had been banished, it would also operate as a bogeyman frightening the Tersians themselves, both those who lived in stone houses on the hill and those in the new city (more and more of whom now reside in one of the up-to-date socialistic five-story apartment buildings, sorts of prefab structures resembling prison cells of gray concrete). As time went on, however, the Mahalla of the Damned began also to play a somewhat consolatory role. When fear tyrannized the Tersians both day and night, especially during the frightening period of the purges against "internal enemies," they whispered to each other, glancing in that direction with terrified eyes, "Things stink for us, but let's not forget that lousier exists," as one said, to which another whispered, "Yes, yes, you're right, misery has no bottom." Now, with the regime's fall, those exiled in the rusty shacks have been replaced by Gypsies who come to Ters from surrounding areas. Tersians have given the Mahalla of the Damned a new name; it is now called Kingdom of the Gypsies.

• ■ •

The hearse left the Avenue de l'Europe after about a quarter of an hour, turning left into the Rue des Âmes, a very narrow street full of potholes. This road passed in front of the Kingdom of the Gypsies and continued directly to Ters's cemetery. On both sides of the Rue des Âmes were jaded, senile trees that never blossomed no matter what the season.

Fatmira P.'s father signaled the driver, who stopped. Those behind stopped without understanding why. Fatmira's father nodded with his head toward the Kingdom of the Gypsies. Karl then looked that way and saw a well-dressed couple who were approaching the hearse with rapid steps. Both were

Gypsies: a man about 40 years old holding a clarinet in his hand and a woman of about 30 with curly hair that fell upon her shoulders. The man with the clarinet was wearing a black suit with a white bow tie. The woman wore a black fur coat and high-heeled boots that accentuated her shapely legs.

The two performers expressed greetings with a slight nod, without speaking.

Karl smiled at the woman with the curly hair.

"They are musicians. They'll join us. Our daughter dreamed of becoming a singer," said Rustem to Karl and Crazy Pandi.

The hearse continued its progress on the Rue des Âmes with the two additional people in the minuscule funeral procession that followed.

• ▪ •

"Where are you living now, Karl?"

Karl at first considered this some sort of auditory deception, but he soon realized that the inquiry had come from the mouth of Crazy Pandi. They were walking slowly behind the hearse, one next to the other. Hunched over as he was, with cane in hand, Crazy Pandi seemed to have addressed his question more to the ground than to Karl. In addition, this was only the second time in Karl's life that he had heard Crazy Pandi speak, the first time being approximately an hour earlier, when Pandi expressed his condolences to Fatmira's parents.

"In America," Karl replied.

"I'd like so much to see America before I die," said Crazy Pandi, ejecting the words with difficulty from his mouth, as though he were someone with a toothache.

"You did well in leaving Ters, Karl," Crazy Pandi said after a bit.

"Thank you," said Karl. He thought at once that this "thank you" he had mumbled in answer, just because a person suggested he had done well in leaving Ters, was somewhat idiotic.

"I love Ters in spite of everything," continued Crazy Pandi. "Do you know, Karl, why I love it? Because it has never done harm to anyone, only to itself."

Crazy Pandi lifted his cane slightly as though indicating to the coffin that the cemetery lay ahead of them. He then said, "People are everywhere the same, Karl. The same lunacies, the same fears, the same manias, the same dreams. What changes are only the amounts, from place to place, city to city."

• ■ •

In the countyard to Slaughterhouse Bossio, exactly opposite the cemetery's entrance, Fatmira P.'s funeral procession was greeted by a surprise. A mass of about 35 Tersians who were there had come to blows. Karl and the others had heard their inarticulate cries from a distance and the man with the clarinet had indeed supposed that the noise was coming from hunters who trained their dogs in the Slaughterhouse courtyard. However, when the hearse approached the cemetery's entrance, the man with the clarinet and the others stared goggle-eyed at the peculiar spectacle in the courtyard and words froze like stalagmites in their mouths.

• ■ •

Whoever knows Ters thoroughly is aware that its inhabitants are distinguished for insatiable curiosity. Thus a group of Tersians, urged on by this curiosity, had decided to spy secretly on Fatmira P.'s funeral. It appears that they did not wish to miss that utterly unheard-of event, the first boycotted funeral in Ters's history. To occupy a privileged position for stealthy observation and at the same time to remain unobserved, the snooping group had hidden behind three large cypress trees next to Slaughterhouse Bossio.

However, while these folks were waiting for Fatmira P.'s hearse to appear, two black Mercedes sedans appeared in the Slaughterhouse courtyard, both of which were filled with the Concrete Boss's hooligans — namely, eight young, muscular, black-suited men with half-shaven heads. Their mission was to guarantee by any means that Fatmira P.'s funeral should be boycotted. Perhaps everything would have been written very differently if the hooligans had not accidentally discovered the group of Tersians the moment when one of the hooligans moved away to urinate in a corner of the Slaughterhouse courtyard. This one, having perceived these Tersians watching from behind the tall cypress trees, approached the curious group, ready to bully them. The moment he recognized among them Ladi the Cinnamon (owner of the cinnamon shop in the center of town), he insulted Ladi's sister. In Ters one says, "It's better to kill a Tersian than to insult his sister." This affront was the spark that inaugurated the violent, irrational conflagration that followed.

When the hooligan saw himself suddenly surrounded by the exasperated glances of the

Tersian group, he called upon his friends for help. These poured out of their two black Mercedes sedans like famished mongrels. Shoves, wallops, maledictions, punches, and insults mixing with one another became a hopeless tangle. The group of curious Tersians, both men and women, instead of becoming frightened by the hooligans' charge, grew still more bellicose, resembling now an army platoon.

Amid the ensuing tumult, five or six stray dogs that had found refuge in the Slaughterhouse came out to hobnob with the aggravated crowd, wagging their filthy tails. With perplexed eyes, the dogs watched these humans who were hollering and cussing. And the moment when one of the hooligans took out his pistol to shoot blindly, one of the dogs, the largest of all, pounced on him maniacally and buried its teeth into his calf. The hooligan let out from his mouth a scream that took your breath away, mixed with insults and curses. Then, with a quick turn of his body, he aimed the pistol toward the dog and emptied three bullets into its back. The animal fell down in a heap like a stone, emitting from its mouth a howl of complaint like that of a choking infant. Blood beginning to run from the dog's body mixed with the hooligan's human blood, creating a small red pool thereabouts. At that moment, as though this blood had taken hold of both Tersians and dogs, they all ran amuck upon the eight hooligans with punches, yelping, stones, pieces of wood, like a military platoon in perfectly synchronized movements.

• ■ •

"Let those madmen kill each other," said Crazy Pandi, attempting to bring back to reality the funeral procession's stunned members. The four men, this time without the help of Crazy Pandi, lifted Fatmira P.'s coffin out of the hearse. Beneath human shouts and canine growls, carrying the coffin on their shoulders, they passed through the cemetery's entrance.

As soon as the coffin was positioned next to the open grave, three young women emerged from the vehement human tangle in the Slaughterhouse courtyard. Straightening their clothing and fixing their messy hair, they joined without any gestures or words the others around the coffin.

"Shall we begin?" asked in a soft voice the Gypsy singer with the curly hair and black fur coat.

"Yes," replied Fatmira P.'s father, his face hard and inexpressive.

The Gypsy man squeezed the clarinet's mouthpiece between his lips while the woman with the curly hair took a deep breath. Karl expected to hear some sort of dirge, but the singer began a well-known love song that the Tersians sing even at weddings. Her voice, warm and deep, spread like a silken cloak over the surrounding tombs:

I have days to see you,
my sweet-smelling flower.
Oh my dear, at your window
I wait years for your sake.
Ach, my moon, you
cross Ters all alone.
Smelling of fresh roses and drunken light,
see how you make young men
dizzy day and night.

A deep silence fell when the song ended.

"May memory of her be eternal!" was heard from the voices around the tomb, like a refrain ending the song.

"The time has come for us to say goodbye, my daughter," said Rustem, Fatmira's father, bending over the coffin and caressing it with his palms.

• ■ •

Now, death smells. I mean death has a special smell, over and above the smell of cyanide, cordite, blood, carrion, or burned flesh. It is a gray smell: stops the heart and cuts off the breath. The smell of empty bodies . . .[10]

Karl thought of that entire excerpt in English. He repeated it silently, also in English. During his five years in America, he had suffered from the fact that he still did not manage to think (or dream) in English. His dreams in America were in Albanian, Greek, French, Spanish . . . , even in Russian. English still refused to become his own. Only at this moment in the cemetery of Ters, seeing the coffin descend into the tomb's dark mouth, did Karl catch himself thinking in English with an ease, certainty, and composure that he had never previously experienced. Reaching his ears were the shouts of the passionate crowd in the Slaughterhouse courtyard, the furious dog-yelping, the sobbing of Falma, Fatmira's mother. Tears then began to flow also from Karl's eyes. The last time he had wept was at

10. Excerpt from William Burrroughs's song "The Name Is Clem Snide."

his mother's funeral many years earlier, before he left Ters. He did not weep at his father's funeral. Yet now, saying farewell for the last time to an unfamiliar girl, next to people who were almost unknown to him, with the peculiar Slaughterhouse crowd of Tersians in the background, Karl wept without being able to control his tears. Fragmentary images like changing reflections in a kaleidoscope began to pass through his brain: he and Kleio making love in the Train Room, he and Frederik reading excerpts from the *Communist Manifesto* in front of their enthusiastically applauding parents, the downcast eyes of Tower of Babel telling him, "Karl, go far away from Ters as soon as you can," the frightened eyes of Christos P. in Athens telling Karl the same regarding Greece (because in such countries people continue to view migration as salvation, continue to believe more in the kindness of foreigners than in their homeland's justice), the picture of himself bathed in blood after he had been assaulted in Athens, the threat "We'll bury you alive, filthy Albanian," Frederik's frenzy and the word "traitor" bellowed at him that morning before his brother slammed the door directly in his face, the note from his mother with a heart drawn by her deformed hands, Klodi and himself at Mount Auburn Cemetery and the question tormenting him regarding where he would like his grave to be when he died, the slogan on Fatmira's apartment house, "Whores destroy families," written posthaste with loathing, the photo of Fatmira on the wall just a few weeks before her death, and again the verses he had written after meeting Kleio in Omonoia Square in Athens:

po të vije si një mëkat / If you came like a sin
do të prisja si një falje / I would meet you as a pardon
po të vije aq e trishtë si një rrenojë / If you came so sad like a ruin
do të prisja si një strehë / I would meet you as a shelter.

THE END

Biographies

GAZMEND KAPLLANI is an Albanian-born polyglot author, journalist, and scholar. He lived in Athens, Greece for over 20 years (1991–2012), studying philosophy and psychology at the National and Kapodistrian University of Athens and receiving his Ph.D. in political science and history from Panteion University. He was one of the most outspoken journalists in the Greek press regarding migrants and minorities.

He is the author of two collections of poetry in Albanian and four published novels (written in Greek and Albanian). His literary work centers on borders, totalitarianism, migration, identity, and how Balkan history has shaped private and public narratives and memories. His books are taught in prestigious universities in Europe, the United States, and Canada and have been the subject of many scholarly essays.

Kapllani's first best-selling novel, *A Short Border Handbook* (2006), has been translated and published into 10 languages so far. It has been adapted for the stage by Bornholm Theater in Denmark and The National Theater of the Deaf in Greece. It won the International Literary Prize of the City of Cassino in Italy in 2017. His three other novels, *My Name is Europe, The Last Page,* and *Wrongland,* have been published so far in French, Italian, Albanian, Greek, and English; *The Last Page* was short-listed for the French Cezam Prix Littéraire Inter CE 2016 and awarded the literary prize of the Salon du Livre des Balkans in Paris, France. *Wrongland* was adapted for the stage by the Greek theater director Pantelis Flatsousis and performed in Athens, Greece, in 2022.

Since 2012 Kapllani has been living in the United States, where he was a fellow at the Radcliffe Institute for Advanced Study at Harvard University and writer-in-residence at Brown University and Wellesley College. He taught creative writing and (Southeastern) European history at Emerson College in Boston, MA (2013–2018). Gazmend Kapllani and his wife Sonia currently live in Chicago, IL, where he directs the Hidai "Eddie" Bregu Endowment in Albanian Studies at DePaul University and the DePaul Albanian and Southeastern European Studies Program.

PETER BIEN, educated at Deerfield, Harvard, Haverford, and Columbia, professed English literature at Dartmouth College from 1961 to 1997 but had become involved earlier with Modern Greek literature owing to his marriage in 1955 to a native Greek whom he met in England when both were at the Quaker study center Woodbrooke. His translations of Nikos Kazantzakis's *The Last Temptation of Christ* appeared in 1960, of *Saint Francis* in 1962, *Report to Greco* in 1965, and *Zorba the Greek* in 2014. He also translated Stratis Myrivilis's *Life in the Tomb* (1977), a poetry book by Myron Zolotakis (2023), and two poetry collections by S. S. Harkianakis (2013, 2021). A coauthored series of textbooks for learning Modern Greek culminated with *Greek Today* (2004). His scholarly studies include *L. P. Hartley* (1963), *Kazantzakis and the Linguistic Revolution in Greek Literature* (1972), *Three Generations of Greek Writers: Introductions to Cavafy, Kazantzakis, Ritsos* (1983), *Kazantzakis: Politics of the Spirit* (2 vols., 1989 and 2007), and *Yannis Ritsos: Collected Studies & Translations* (2011). He also collected, chose, and translated *The Selected Letters of Nikos Kazantzakis* (2012). He taught as a visiting professor at the universities of Harvard, Princeton, Columbia, Brown, Melbourne, Thessaloniki twice, and Crete. A cofounder and past president of the Modern Greek Studies Association of America and Canada, he served as editor of the association's *Journal of Modern Greek Studies* from 1991 to 1999. He has been honored by the E. Harris Harbison Award for Distinguished Teaching (Danforth Foundation, 1968), three Fulbright Fellowships, and an honorary doctorate from the Aristotle University of Thessaloniki (2007).